This book is dedicated to:
LUCKY
DUCHESS
AND
GEORGE
WHO WERE MY INSPIRATION FOR CHANCE
THEY LIVE ON IN MY MEMORY AND HEART.

Excerpt from Kahlil Gibran
You would know the secret of death.
But how shall you find it unless you seek it in the heart of life?
The owl whose night-bound eyes are blind unto the day cannot unveil
the mystery of light.
If you would indeed behold the spirit of death, open your heart wide
unto the body of life.
For life and death are one, even as the river and the sea are one.

CHAPTER ONE

Located at the top of a long winding mountain range, Mum's hometown of Balford looked picturesque in the cool, still, morning air. A thin cloudy mist cloaked the earth and drifted upwards to cover the hills. Soon the summer sun would make its way over the top of the tallest trees, dissolve the fog and end the chilly beginning to the day.

Like many small and not so small towns, the bakery and newsagent were open. Early risers and tradesmen were buying bread, coffee or breakfast, and whatever else they needed to kick start their day.

I parked the car and waited in line at the bakery. My hungry stomach grumbled in response to the scent of various mouth-watering aromas. Excitement had prevented me from eating before commencing the last hour of my long journey. The promise of a new life waited for me at my grandmother's house and I had been eager to start my day.

Gathering up my order of a coffee and meat pie, I sat at one of the tables provided at the front of the bakery. Slowly, the town came to life as more people filled the streets to go about the business of their lives.

An old couple sitting at the table next to me, eyed me for a while until the woman spoke, 'Are you just passing through, dear?'

After Balford, the road headed west into the outback, so I knew the question was loaded with curiosity.

'No. I've inherited a property here. If I like it, I'll stay here.'

Or not. I guess that depends on what I find. Poor Mum. She was so convinced that those hallucinations about the house being a gateway for the dead were real.

'Which property would that be?' The woman's voice intruded on my troubled thoughts.

Taking a sip of coffee to delay my answer, I decided there was no harm to her questions, and it might be a good way to judge the local's opinion of my grandmother, or if they knew of her.

'Vivienne Legg was my grandmother. It's her property that I've inherited.'

The stillness that settled over the couple was unmistakable. They shared a glance full of meaning. The woman replaced her coffee on the table with a carefulness that spoke of shock, and a need to steady her nerves. The man cleared his throat with a loud harrumph.

'The Legg women have been an important part of this community for generations,' the man said. 'Do you ... intend to follow in your grandmother's footsteps?'

Why the hesitation? The Legg women? Plural? Were there no men? Follow in her footsteps?

'Ah. Um, I'm not sure what you mean. What did my grandmother do?'

'You must be Vera's daughter,' the woman said.

Which I thought dodged the question nicely.

'You knew my mother?' I asked, following her lead. If she didn't want to talk about my grandmother, that was fine. Mum hadn't wanted to speak of her either.

'We went to school with her. I'm Ernie Milledge, and this is my wife Beatrice,' replied the man.

Finally! Someone who knew my family. I smiled at them. 'I'm Sandrine. Pleased to meet you,'

'Sandrine? What an unusual name!' Exclaimed Beatrice. 'Er, I mean ... usually,' she faltered uncomfortably.

'I know,' I intervened before the poor woman dug a deeper hole for herself. 'What can I say, Mum liked the name, and I'm stuck with it.'

Though I wished I had let her finish. What had she meant by 'usually'?

'Yes. Of course. I'm so sorry dear. How impertinent of me,' apologised Beatrice before continuing. 'How is Vera? We haven't seen her for a very long time.'

Pain, along with irritation, flared within me. I let the question lay unanswered for several heartbeats, her prying was obvious, but I didn't want to snap at the woman.

'Mum died four months ago, from cancer,' I told her, relieved at the normality of my tone.

'We're very sorry to hear that,' replied Ernie in a quiet voice, staring at the table.

Beatrice frowned at him and turned her attention to me.

'Did your mother not tell you what your grandmother does er did?' She hastily corrected.

'Mum never spoke of her. I thought she was dead until a couple of months before Mum died.'

'What a shame.' Outrage was clear in Beatrice Milledge's voice. 'Vivienne was a *wonderful* woman. She was very much loved and revered in this community. Vera should never have run out on her the way she did.'

'That's enough, Beatrice,' her husband interceded, his voice sharp. 'The girl doesn't need to hear town gossip.'

Beatrice sniffed, opened her mouth and closed it again. Obviously, there was more she wanted to say, but Ernie's rebuke and his continuing glare inhibited her.

Like a grey cloud, disappointment settled over me. Mum's refusal to speak of her mother and her childhood hinted at secrets and fear. Whatever I had hoped I might learn from talking to the locals, scattered like leaves before a turbulent wind. I returned to sipping my coffee and picking at the meat pie. My hunger seemed to have left me.

Chairs scraped on pavement as Beatrice and Ernie rose to leave. A work-roughened hand placed a piece of paper on the table, and Beatrice said softly, 'If you ever want to talk, this is my number, dear.'

I took the note and nodded at her, though I doubted she was the right person to help me understand Mum's need to flee from her own mother, or whatever it was she had really fled from.

CHAPTER TWO

During a brief exploration of the town, I made a booking for two nights in a motel I discovered and set out to find Harriet Gould's office. I'd received a letter from Harriet, a solicitor, four months after I returned to my family home to care for Mum during the last stages of her battle with cancer. The letter informed me of my grandmother's death and that I'd inherited her property in Far North Queensland.

That would have been fine, except at the time I was unaware I had a grandmother.

My father's parents died in a car accident not long after he was born. Dad's aunt and uncle raised him, though he preferred to treat them as if they didn't exist. Like so much of Dad's life, that door remained closed to me, and I never met them.

When I asked Mum about them, her reply had been, 'Believe me, Sandrine. They're not people you'd want in your life.'

Any further questions were answered with a shake of her head and a firm, 'No'.

According to Mum, her mother had died before she went to university, where she met Dad. But I held the proof of that lie in my hands, and ill or not, I wanted answers from her while she was still alive.

I waited until Mum had eaten, was rested, and appeared to be relatively pain free - then I read the letter to her.

'Why? Mum, why would you lie? Your mother was alive until a couple of months ago? I could have known her. Why would you....?'

The moan, that escaped her lips, became a quickly suppressed scream. A jolt of surprise and alarm clutched at my throat, closing it mid question.

'No! No! She can't do this! She can't do this to you. You mustn't Sandrine! Burn the letter! Burn it! Give it to me!'

Mum reached out one scrawny, feeble hand as if to snatch the letter from my grasp. I moved backwards in the chair I was sitting in, easily evading her clutching hand.

'You don't understand,' she wailed. Tears filled her eyes, and distress scored the lines of her face into deeper furrows.

'No. You're right, I don't.' My tone softened. 'But you should have explained it to me. I haven't been a child for a very long time.'

'You wouldn't have believed me. Even now, I know you won't believe me. You will think I'm making it all up, that I'm lying. It's so....' Her eyes closed, and her voice quieted so suddenly, I could barely hear her. 'I can't find the words,' she finished.

A few moments later, Mum's eyes opened to stare into mine, 'I wanted to protect you. I just wanted to protect you. You have no idea,' she moaned softly.

'Mum. Please stop worrying. I don't know what I'm going to do. I have this house, and a lot of other things to deal with. But right now, I have you to take care of.'

The conflicting emotions flitting across Mum's face were difficult to interpret, fear and sadness appeared to be the dominant ones.

Reaching out to grab my arm with a surprisingly strong grip, she said in a voice filled with anxiety, 'Sell it. Don't go there. Whatever you do, don't go there.'

My stomach muscles clenched in response to the anxiety I heard in her voice.

'Why not?' I asked, trying to keep my voice calm and my face unreadable.

'Because .... No! You mustn't go Sandrine. Promise me you won't go there.'

'Tell me why first, and then I'll think about it.'

'I can't tell you. You wouldn't believe me even if I did.'

Mum closed her eyes; it was her way of ending the conversation. I sat with her and watched as she sunk slowly into sleep, then I phoned the solicitor to explain my situation. Harriet Gould promised me she would supervise the care of the property, until I was able to take possession of it.

A quick shake of my head cleared the memory from my mind, and I paused to take a steadying breath before I entered the solicitor's office.

Introductions and pleasantries over; Ms Gould, from behind her wide desk, studied me with sharp, assessing dark brown eyes. Her once black hair was filled with broad, white streaks. From our phone calls, I had envisioned a younger woman, instead I suspected she was nearer my grandmother's age. Her smooth dark, coffee coloured skin and features revealed little sign of her true age.

'Vivienne was a very dear friend of mine. What do you know of your grandmother?' Her voice wasn't harsh, but there was no welcome in her tone.

'Nothing,' I told her, matching her manner. She was not going to intimidate me, if that was her goal.

'Your mother told you *nothing*?' Her tone was incredulous.

'Like I told you when I first phoned you. I didn't even know I had a grandmother. Mum always told me she was dead.'

Harriet's lips tightened in what I took to be disapproval, then she said, 'I loved your grandmother like a sister, she was strong, but I think Vera needed more gentle handling, and your grandmother could never see that.'

'I don't know what went on between Mum and my grandmother. Mum never spoke of her, even up to her death she would never explain.'

Which wasn't strictly true. Mum had eventually given me an explanation of sorts, but it was one filled with fantasy brought on by pain and the drugs needed to control that pain. I didn't feel the need to share that with this forceful stranger.

'Do you intend to stay?' asked Ms Gould, interrupting my thoughts.

'I don't know. I want to have a look at the place before I make that decision.'

'What about your home in Victoria?'

'I sold it.'

For some reason, this information softened her attitude.

'Good. In that case it's unlikely that you'll return. I'll read the will, then there will be papers for you to sign. Vivienne has also left you a good deal of money ....'

I heard her voice but not the words. I had experienced all that was required with wills and the settling of property with Mum and Dad's recent deaths.

Instead, my mind was revisiting my early morning conversation with the Milledge's. From what they'd said, and not said, I had the distinct impression Harriet Gould did not share their opinion of Mum and my grandmother. Vivienne had been obviously well liked, and a respected and valued member of the community. Mum's flight from the area (or her mother, I couldn't decide which), was viewed very differently. If she was going to be unsympathetic towards Mum, I wasn't sure I wanted to see Beatrice Milledge again. Yet I sensed there were secrets, and like Mum, they seemed to want to keep them hidden.

Harriet pushing a key, that looked like it had been forged in another era, towards me, focused my attention on her once again. I looked down to see that she had also included a map.

'If you decide to stay and have any questions, you have my card. Have you heard a word I said?'

'Not really,' I replied truthfully. 'Mum and Dad died within eighteen months of each other. After settling both their affairs, I believe I am familiar with all that is entailed.'

'Mm. Well, it is apparent to me that you have Vivienne's strength. I warned her often enough, but she never took my advice. Whether you want to hear it or not, I'm going to tell you the same thing I told her. When you have more strength than most people, first you must choose kindness.'

She paused to give me an even sterner look, which until that moment I hadn't thought possible, before continuing, 'Above all, Sandrine, choose love when dealing with others, especially with family.

If Vivienne had chosen kindness and love, I believe Vera would have stayed, or at the very least, returned.'

Lips pursed, she paused long enough to submit me to another close scrutiny before continuing, 'And you would understand the true legacy of what you have inherited,' she finished cryptically.

Before I had the presence of mind to ask her to unravel that strange remark, Harriet Gould ushered me to the door and I found myself standing on the pavement, clutching an old key and a map I knew I would have difficulty reading.

I walked away from that ferocious old woman's office, determined to find a hot tub to soak in, a delicious meal with a glass of wine, and to have a good night's sleep, before making any attempt to find my grandmother's place.

CHAPTER THREE

My journey north to the property I had inherited from my grandmother began two weeks ago; while I had been in no hurry to reach my destination, something tugged at me, urging me on.

Following the inland highway, the seldom-empty road stretched between small country towns populated by farming communities, and bustling regional centres. The road traversed a changing landscape of bushland filled with a variety of iron bark, eucalyptus, bottlebrush and trees for which I had no name.

At times, I lingered to explore places that caught my interest; staying longer to enjoy meals created by country cooks who used fresh produce to deliver delicious meals and tempting deserts. Other times, compelled by unseen forces to leave the inland road, I headed towards the coast, where I walked sandy beaches and watched wild waves crash against the shore.

Generated by the sorrow that Mum's last days had been filled with the horrible fantasy that her family home was a gateway for the dead, the roaring surf seemed to mirror the conflict I carried within me.

The beaches in North Queensland, thanks to the barrier reef hugging its coastline, were peaceful. Inexplicably, my mood changed to match the serenity of the seas. Able to breathe more easily, I was glad I'd resisted the urge to give into Mum's begging.

Leaving behind the life I knew had been hard, but there was nothing to keep me tethered to the place where I grew up. My grandmother's place beckoned, and I was keen to see and explore Mum's childhood home and hopefully discover something of my family history.

In the space of almost two years. I'd lost both my parents and Robert, the man I thought I loved and with whom I had spent six years.

Dad's sudden death from a heart attack had been a shock.

More shocking was his funeral.

Mum and I sat side by side as over a hundred strangers poured into the church to pay their last respects.

'He was a wonderful man. He never missed a Sunday service,' a woman told Mum, then added, 'It's a shame you never came with him.'

There was a definite bite to her words that gave a lie to the smiling face.

'Well, that's news to us. And we might have done if only he had asked,' I told her, not bothering to keep the sting from my voice, or the censure from my face. She'd looked at me askance and moved hurriedly away.

'He saved my life. You were so lucky to have him as a father,' another woman I'd never met told me tearfully at the graveside. 'My father left when I was twelve. Mum and I never saw him again.'

'Well ...,' I began, and Mum nudged me into silence.

That moment was not the time to tell this stranger my father hadn't physically left, but he had never connected with me emotionally.

As a doctor, Dad spent all his working life looking after other people. He, Mum, and I shared a house, not our lives. My parents had separate bedrooms; something I accepted as a child, but as I grew older and ventured into the homes of friends, I came to realise the relationship my parents shared differed a great deal from those of my friends.

Dad came and went like a well-kept border. His clothes were washed, ironed, and put away in his cupboard. Meals of his choice were prepared and kept warm for him. He came home, ate alone, slept alone, and would go out into the world to do whatever he wanted – alone. He barely spoke to either Mum or me. We lived our lives together without him.

What I mostly remembered from his funeral; was how numb I felt. Yet at the same time, I recognised that deep inside, a part of me wanted to scream at these strangers and tell them that the man they admired so much, was not the man I knew.

In contrast, Mum's funeral consisted of myself and a few of our friends. She died after a short skirmish with a cancer so advanced it defeated her before she even had a chance to fight.

Robert came to the funeral, he hugged me and for a brief moment I clung to him, then broke contact and turned away. I shrugged off the hold he had on my arm as I turned, and felt him step back, which told me he knew that there was not an 'us' anymore. His selfish refusal to help my mother when she needed it the most had been the turning point, and the end of our six-year relationship.

At one time, we tried having children together, when I failed to fall pregnant, as if in a secret, shared relief, neither of us pursued the reason for our apparent infertility. Yet I stayed with him. In hindsight, I realised I wanted the connection to another person more than I wanted to be true to what I knew and who I was.

That was until Mum became ill and needed constant care.

'Allow the professionals to look after her,' he had urged.

'Don't be so insulting, I *am* a professional, Robert.' I told him coldly.

Robert held me by the arms, rubbing his hands up and down as if to soothe me.

'I know that honey. I'm sure you're a wonderful nurse to other people. It will be different with your mother, more emotional. If Vera is in a palliative care unit, she'll have around the clock care, and it won't drain you. You can visit her as much as you want. Not only that, think of how it will affect our lives. You will be at her beck and call twenty-four hours a day, there will be no time for us.'

I stepped back, pulling away from him and his selfishness.

'And if it were me?' I demanded. 'Would you put me into care, or would you look after me?'

Robert fell silent, his too handsome face and cool blue eyes told me he was searching for an answer that would reassure me - and came up with zilch.

He took a deep breath, opened his mouth, and closed it again. 'Sandy, please,' he pleaded softly.

'Goodbye Robert,' I told him.

CHAPTER FOUR

The shock of discovering I'd inherited a house and land from a grandmother who I never knew existed, had subsided. However, it still bothered me that she'd been alive until a year ago. I doubted that I would ever understand why Mum lied to me about her mother being dead.

If she'd told me the truth, maybe I wouldn't have been deep in the bush of Far North Queensland, standing in the middle of a dirt road, perusing a map that I'd studied numerous times over the past couple of hours.

'Sandy, my girl,' I muttered, 'I think that solicitor has sent you on a wild goose chase.'

Wiping my hot, damp face on my sleeve, I pulled at my shirt where sweat had stuck it uncomfortably to my body.

Frustrated and doing my best not to scream, I'd stopped the car, grabbed the map and a bottle of water, and stepped out into a heat that covered me like a heavy wet blanket. Towering eucalypts provided thin shade. I retrieved my hat from the passenger seat and plonked it on my head.

Summer's heat dragged at my already depleted energy levels. I'd spent a sleepless night replaying, over and over in my head, the conversations I'd had with the Milledge's and Harriet Gould. The things that I sensed were not said bothered me the most.

The grit of tiredness lingered in my eyes. Annoying clouds of tiny, black, sticky bush flies bombarded me in an effort to attach themselves to my face. My arm acted like a metronome as I constantly waved them away.

Taking a swig from the water bottle, I glanced around the countryside. From the new shoots of green grass losing their battle with the prevailing heat, it appeared that rain had fallen recently. The parched land had drunk its fill and returned the earth to dust.

The mournful cry of the black cockatoo sounded above my head. I lifted my gaze and watched the flocks' graceful flight. For a moment, peace settled over me, until I turned my attention back to the map and the track meandering through the trees.

Did Harriet Gould give me the wrong bloody map on purpose? The thought wandered into my mind, and I pushed it away.

I turned the map upside down, but it still didn't make any sense.

Blasted maps why are they so hard to read?

Because you can't read maps. Said a small voice somewhere deep in the back of my head, which I immediately ignored.

Irritation had me grinding my teeth and blowing air through my nose. I resisted the urge to crumple the piece of paper and throw it as far away as I possibly could.

She must have given me the wrong map!

There's no reasonable explanation why she would do that.

Now I was arguing with myself. Great!

Letting the hand that held the map fall to my side; I stared, first one way and then the other, down the narrow dusty road I'd followed backwards and forwards since early morning. The trail (it was a bit of a stretch to call it a road), snaked through the bush leading to several isolated properties in the area - none of which were my grandmother's house.

According to the map, the dirt road I was on was a thoroughfare that eventually connected to the Bruce Highway. It also showed the road to the property as plainly marked. In reality, there were numerous bush tracks leading to heaven knew where.

A signpost, clearly indicated on the map, showed the marker as being four kilometres from my grandmother's house. I had discovered the broken sign hiding amongst a tall shrub, and four kilometres from that point was nothing but bush.

Since leaving the main road over two hours ago, I hadn't seen another soul. There were a few buildings set a long way back from the gateways I drove past, though it was difficult to determine if they were houses, sheds, or ruins.

Once more, I thought, studying the map, *and then I'm going back to the motel. I'm sick of driving around aimlessly.*

'Looking for something, girlie?'

I yelped in fright and swung towards the voice. An elderly man stood a couple of metres away.

Where had he come from? And so silently?

I glared at him to cover my alarm at his sudden and soundless appearance.

'You frightened me,' I accused.

He didn't reply. We studied each other without speaking. Thin tufts of grey-flecked brown hair were sticking out from under a felt hat. He wore baggy cotton trousers, and a rough work shirt hung loosely on his wiry frame. Calm brown eyes met mine, and the wild beating of my heart steadied.

I waited a moment longer for him to speak.

He held his unnerving silence, so indicating the map, I showed him the road to my grandmother's house.

He gave me a sharp look. 'Ah, you'd be looking for Violet's Place,' he said. 'It's about time someone came to look after things. The house has gone to ruin since the old lady died.'

It was on the tip of my tongue to tell him my grandmother's name was Vivienne, when he waved his arm in the direction I had come.

'Go back and turn left at the next dirt road, the tree beside it is marked with a circle. Follow that track for a couple of miles, (not kilometres I noted) until you come to a gate. You'll be able to the see the house from there.'

He paused, 'Though you might be better off going back to where you came from, girlie.'

A frisson of alarm speared through me, was he warning or threatening me? And calling me girlie was just plain bloody annoying.

'I'm hardly a girl ....' The retort died on my lips when the old man turned and walked away.

I took another swig of water and watched as he strolled up the road, where puffs of dirt marked his passing.

Back in my car, I looked into the rear vision mirror and caught a final glimpse of him before he disappeared from view.

Grumpy old sod. Probably an old loner who doesn't like the thought of having a neighbour, which I supposed I could be, if the house wasn't a ruin. Please God, don't let him be right. I don't want to have come all this way for nothing, and it would be so nice to have my own home again.

A three-point turn had the car going in the opposite direction. I drove back down the road; over an ancient timber bridge I had driven over several times; all the while keeping an eye out for the tree with a circle and the next dirt track on my left.

I found a tree with what may have been a circle once, now it looked like a misshapen scar. The dirt track before the blemished tree stretched the imagination to say it was a road of any kind. No wonder I'd missed it.

My car wasn't made for bush tracks. I eased it slowly and carefully over the bumps and dips until the gate the old man had spoken of came into view.

Exiting the car, I made my way to the heavy, galvanised iron gate. A metal chain connected the gate to the adjoining post, and held it shut.

Leaning on the gate, I stared at my inheritance, and the memory of Mum's pleading voice weaved its way through my mind.

'After I'm gone, don't go and look at it. Please Sandrine. Please. Promise me you won't go and try to find it.'

Diagnosed with advanced bowel cancer, the ensuing months saw the vigorous, vibrant woman I knew fade slowly and inexorably until the inevitable was a last breath away. It still pained me to remember that her final hours were spent begging me not to go to my grandmother's house.

Once again, in my mind, as I had so often in the past weeks, I saw the tears as they gathered in her eyes and trickled slowly down her face. She struggled to prop herself up and when that failed, she reached out her hand to me. I clasped it gently in my own. Her bones showed clearly under the frail skin.

'You *must* promise me,' she insisted.

We'd had this same conversation many times before, and Mum never offered up the reason she was so unrelenting.

'Tell me why,' I asked softly.

'You won't believe me if I tell you.'

It was a statement she'd often repeated, but I figured if she didn't tell me, then she wouldn't know if I believed her or not.

Feebly, Mum tugged at the hand that lay in my grasp. I released her and she lay back with a sigh that spoke volumes. I sat with her for a while, and we let silence fall between us. I never regretted giving up my job as a nurse to care for Mum, though the past few months had been both extremely hard and very rewarding all at the same time.

A small bell resting on her bedside table allowed Mum to call if she needed me in the middle of the night, or if I wasn't nearby. Stoic in her handling of the pain and discomfort, she hardly ever used it. However, my subconscious mind was tuned into the slightest tinkle and in the early hours of one morning, I awoke to that sound.

'Mum? What's wrong?'

She was awake and appeared alert and stronger than usual.

Briefly, her gaze roved over me, then she indicated the chair with a slight movement of her hand.

For several moments after I was seated her gaze turned inwards, and I was beginning to worry when she spoke.

'It's a gateway for the dead.'

'Pardon? What is?'

'The *house*, Sandrine,' there was a tartness to her voice. 'The house I grew up in. The house my mother has gifted to you. It's not a gift. It's a curse. The dead travel through it to ...,' she shook her head, 'I don't know where they go, but it's a gateway, and it terrified me as a child. Mum only saw the dead. She couldn't talk to them the way I could. I could also see who and what came for them.'

She looked at me, her gaze clear and strong. There was no sign of the dullness of strong drugs in her eyes. But she saw disbelief in mine and gave a short, sharp harrumph.

'I knew you wouldn't believe me.'

'Mum, I ... I know you believe it but talk to me. Tell me what frightened you.'

'Isn't that frightening enough?'

She turned from me. 'Go to bed, Sandrine. I'm sorry I woke you.'

I couldn't think what to say to get her talking again, and my mind couldn't grasp even the idea of a gateway for the dead. It had to be a fantasy, brought on by fentanyl patches and the toxicity of cancer.

Three days later Mum was dead; and in those three days she pleaded with me every day to sell the property without seeing it and never spoke another word about a gateway for the dead.

CHAPTER FIVE

As thoughts of Mum faded from my mind, my eyes gradually focused on my inheritance, or at least what I could see of it. It seemed the old man was right; the land and the buildings did look neglected. Tall trees, surrounding the buildings, cast deep shadows, and all I could make out, was what looked like a few disconnected walls.

Determination, and whatever compulsion had urged me to ignore Mum's appeals, egged me on. Resolved to face whatever came my way, I squared my shoulders, breathed deeply and released the air slowly through my nose. I hadn't come almost the entire length of Eastern Australia to back out now. I wanted to see where Mum had grown up, and I needed to touch something solid that was a connection to the past. Neither Mum nor Dad seemed to need or realise that none of us appeared fully formed and alone – our ancestors walked before us, and it was important to me to catch a glimpse of the life of my only known ancestor.

Stepping through the gate to the property was like opening the fridge door on a hot day. The unexpected coolness lifted my spirits. It didn't matter if the house was uninhabitable; at least the land was mine. I could sell it and buy something else.

Mum might get her wish after all.

With that thought, I pulled the gate wide open, then climbed back into my car. Navigating the smoother track to house, I imagined my small car breathing a sigh of relief. The house took form as I drew near. I was pleased to discover it was not a ruin. From a distance, the shadows from the trees made it seem derelict.

My eyes were drawn to several large fruit trees situated off to the left-hand side, towards the back of the house. The sight of ripe mandarins and oranges, hanging like large carroty balls through a mass of greens leaves, made me realise how hungry I was.

Stopping the car beside the house, I moved towards the orchard. Meandering throughout the grove, I was pleased and amazed by the variety of fruit bearing trees. Selecting a couple of large oranges, I made my way over to a thick old log laying in the shade of a large macadamia tree. Judging by its length, the log had once been a very tall tree. Sitting on the enormous tree trunk, I peeled the oranges, and savoured each sweet, juicy mouthful.

The land around me was flat and appeared to stretch to the horizon in every direction. Tall trees dotted the landscape and birds called to each other. The aroma of the bush in all its complexities ignited my senses; I drew in and released several deep breaths. A sense of peace eased its way into muscles and bones, finally settling into my core. It was the first time I felt anything akin to peace since hearing of Mum's cancer diagnosis.

Movement, on the road, caught my eye. A Ute stopped at the entrance to the property. Its occupant exited the vehicle and stepped through the gate.

From the back of the Ute, two young dogs howled in protest as they watched the man's departure. The first thing I noticed about him, even from that distance was his short black beard and moustache. He stopped for a moment, glanced towards the house and my car, before making his way up the long driveway.

It seemed odd to me that he hadn't driven his car and chose to leave his dogs behind. Though they soon stopped howling and watched his progress with intense interest.

The newcomer approached slowly, almost cautiously, his tall frame moved with all the grace of a large cat. He looked like someone who could look after himself in a fight. As he drew closer, his dark eyes roamed the area, searching for me, I assumed. He clearly had not spotted me.

Sitting in the shade, I remained still, watching him search. Several moments passed before his head turned slowly towards where I was sitting. We stared at each other for a number of heartbeats before he made his way toward me. He seemed unperturbed by my watching him.

He stopped a few feet away. The silence between us held until he finally broke it by saying.

'You're Vivienne's granddaughter.'

It wasn't so much a question as a statement, and I wondered how he had come to that conclusion. But he seemed sure, and there was no use denying something he already knew.

'Sandrine.' I replied, holding out my hand.

'George.' He stepped forward and covered my hand with his own large work roughened one. 'I knew it was something different though I couldn't remember what. Vivienne said you would come.'

'You knew my grandmother? What was she like?'

I ignored the comment about my name. It wasn't like I hadn't heard it before. Whatever had induced Mum to call me such an obscure name I could never fathom. Her reply, when I asked, had been. 'Because it didn't start with a 'V' and I like it. Isn't that enough?' I didn't understand the 'V' reference and she didn't elaborate.

'Like nobody I have ever known,' was his enigmatic reply, which told me precisely nothing, and bought me back to the present and the man standing in front of me.

'So, you had no trouble finding the place?' He asked.

'On the contrary, I had a lot of trouble finding it. If it hadn't been for an old man, I would still be travelling that bloody road. No actually, I wouldn't. I would be back at the hotel enjoying a nice lunch instead of eating oranges. Though they are delicious.' I told him, placing another segment into my mouth.

A jolt of surprise flashed across his face and was gone.

'You've met Rupert?'

Was that alarm or merely surprise I heard in his voice? There was some emotion there I couldn't identify.

I chewed slowly and swallowed, before answering, 'He didn't tell me his name. Strange old man.'

'You don't know the half of it,' he said.

'And are you going to tell me?' I asked.

'In time,' he said mysteriously, then added, 'Well, okay then, if you've met Rupert then it looks like you're going to stay. I told Vivienne I would help you in any way I can.'

'I haven't decided yet if I'm going to stay,' I told him, more than a little annoyed that he took so much for granted.

What was it with the men around here?

'Right.' That one word was loaded with disbelief and amusement. A small grin played around his lips, and he stared at me for several seconds.

'Right,' he said again. Pulling a card from his pocket, he handed it to me. The name on the card was George Lamey.

'I own the farm next door. If you look hard enough, you might be able to see my house amongst the trees. I can see this house ' he paused and added. 'Most of the time anyway. Vivienne used to place a lantern on the verandah if she wanted me. You can call me if your phone works. The electricity can be unreliable here, so if it doesn't work, and if you need help, light a lantern and I'll come.'

Disbelief must have showed on my face. 'Why wouldn't my phone work? I've already checked it, and I can get reception here.'

He didn't answer, just shifted his feet side to side – the only indication that he seemed unsure of what to say.

The silence lengthened until he finally said, 'I know, it doesn't make sense now, but it will in time.' He paused, 'Vivienne said your mum wouldn't explain the house to you. Did she?'

I frowned at him. It couldn't mean what I thought he meant, so I said nothing. Eventually, he dipped his head as if to say goodbye then turned on his heel to walk away.

Abruptly, he turned back.

'*Did* your mother tell you about the house and about Vivienne?'

I opened my mouth, closed it again and pulled a face.

'Mum was dying of cancer when she spoke about the house. Anything she may have told me was done through a drug haze and pain.'

'So, you didn't believe what she told you?'

'No.'

'What did she tell you?'

I considered him for a moment, and decided he would understand that Mum had been hallucinating when she talked about my grandmother.

'She said that it was, um, I'm not sure really … something like a portal that the dead pass through on their way from this life to the next. You do understand, Mum was in a great deal of pain and only operated due to the fentanyl patches that she wore around the clock.'

'Right,' he said. 'Hmm, right.'

It seemed to me that 'right' was his favourite word. It intimated so much and revealed nothing.

He rocked on his heels while staring up into the trees, as if trying to find the right words. 'Hmm. Yes, well keep an open mind.'

With that odd comment, he left without a backward glance.

I watched him walk down the long driveway. He opened and shut the gate, briefly patted his dogs, climbed into his car, and drove away.

CHAPTER SIX

Retrieving the antique skeleton key, Harriet had given me, from the depths of my handbag, I made my way towards the house; a lowset Queenslander made of timber and encircled by a large verandah.

To my surprise, the back door swung open on well-oiled hinges revealing a large, combined kitchen dining room. A hallway was directly in front, and I could see a doorway on either side.

Hesitantly, I stepped inside and found an unwelcome houseguest sitting on the table. Whiskers twitching, the mouse sniffed in my direction, then went on nibbling at whatever it had been eating.

My voice shattered the silence. 'You better find somewhere else to live.'

The tiny rodent paused, sought my scent again and stared at me with an affronted, bewildered expression, as if I were the intruder. Then, with a quick flick of its tail, it disappeared over the side of the table. I didn't see the hole it bolted into but made a mental note to check out all tiny rodent size holes and seal them up.

For a moment, I stood still to get a feel for the place. I let my gaze drift around the room. Apart from the dust which covered every surface, the room was tidy, though it exuded an air of general neglect. There was a sense of waiting and wanting to please; I felt reassured and took a first, tentative step forward. Feeling like an intruder myself, I set out to explore the rest of the house.

Glancing around the kitchen, it appeared as if time had stood still. Heavy timber, free standing cupboards lined one wall. A kitchen sink, with open shelving beneath, sat underneath a window with a view of the orchard. Two small cupboards placed on either side of the sink, provided a small amount of bench space.

Set back into an alcove in the wall, a well preserved, ancient wood stove stood next to a more modern hot water system. I made a mental note to research how to use such a contraption, and to buy a gas stove.

A quick peek into the cupboards revealed all the cutlery, crockery, and cookery I would need, old but in good order and in need of a wash. The fridge definitely required an update.

The doors, on either side of the hallway, opened into two bedrooms.

On a Victorian dressing table in the largest bedroom, obviously my grandmother's, rested a black and white photograph. I studied the woman in the frame then glanced in the mirror. I saw similarly high cheekbones, small button nose and shoulder length hair without a curl in it. I wondered at her colouring. The mirror reflected pale green eyes and dark brown hair. I looked thin and pale - too thin, too pale. I turned away.

On the other side of the hallway past the two bedrooms, I stepped through the open door into a comfortable lounge-room. An old-fashioned treadle sewing machine stood in one corner. From the lounge-room, a door opened onto the front verandah.

Moving outside, I meandered around the large verandah until I found myself at the back door again. I had passed another door further back and retraced my steps. Unlocking it with the same old key I used to open the main door, I tugged on the handle and found it led into a large bathroom that held a claw foot tub, over which hung a shower rose. The room also possessed a toilet and a hand basin. From the bathroom, another door led back into the open plan, kitchen dining room.

I found the laundry in a shed separate to the house; it consisted of an antiquated copper and a cement tub. I groaned, I would have to get a washing machine, there was no way I was going to wash clothes in that.

Except for needing a new fridge, an easier to use stove and a washing machine, I was pleasantly surprised to find the house was fully furnished. Apart from the dust, cobwebs and unwelcome guest, it appeared my grandmother had gone for a holiday and the house was waiting for her to return.

Perhaps it was waiting for me?

The sudden thought gave me a feeling of comfort and belonging, and inexplicably I felt I was home. The tension that had collected in my body, drained away as if a plug had been pulled, and I was glad that I hadn't made any promises to Mum. Whatever her fears, they held no relevance for me.

Relocking all the doors, I returned to my car. In the morning, I could reassure Ms Gould that I would keep the house; and return with whatever I needed to restore the place to a habitable condition.

The sun cast a soft glow across the landscape early the following morning when I returned to the house with cleaning equipment and food. I spent the day removing all traces of dust and cobwebs from the kitchen and dining room. My next target was the main bedroom and the bathroom, then I would move into the house to finish making it my own.

I couldn't bring myself to kill the nest of tiny mice I found tucked away beneath a hole in the floorboards. They could stay until they were old enough to leave home, then I would board up their cubbyhouse.

Or maybe I would get a cat.

The following days passed in a blur of cleaning, buying groceries and settling my few belongings into the house.

George visited with his dogs, who he introduced as Jack, a brown Kelpie, and Sally, a black and white Border Collie. His conversation mainly consisted of showing me how to use the various antiquated apparatus that my grandmother had obviously used in her everyday life.

Despite having a new washing machine, that I was loading with clothes I found in the spare bedroom cupboard, George's latest mission was to give me a detailed set of instructions on how to use the old copper.

I rolled my eyes at him. 'George, as you can see, I have a new washing machine. Why would you think that I wanted to learn to use that old thing?'

Adding detergent, I closed the lid of the machine. I wasn't sure who the clothes were meant for, but something urged me to clean them and place them back in the cupboard.

George gave me a look that was hard to interpret.

'What?' I demanded.

'You'll still need the copper sometimes,' he replied enigmatically, and refused to say more.

I contented myself with rolling my eyes again and wondering about the strange workings of the mind of men. There was no way I was going to use the copper, when a perfectly good and modern, labour-saving device was at my disposal.

The hours turned into days and the days into weeks. The only, though welcome break in my routine were George's weekly visits. Summer moved seamlessly into autumn, a gentle rhythm entered my life and flowed through my days.

Occasionally, I thought I heard Mum's voice and imagined her watching me as I went about my work. Grief can do strange things to a person's mind. Mostly, I was able to ignore these strange experiences and allow the peace that I had found to fill my being.

'Please Sandrine,' Mum's voice interrupted my thoughts.

I decided not to ignore the imaginings going on inside my head.

'What do you want to talk about Mum?' I said aloud.

I'd had many discussions, in my mind, with Mum since her death. Now, I wanted to talk aloud, as if in hearing her voice for myself, I could be sure I was talking to Mum and not imagining the conversation.

'To tell you I'm sorry.'

She sounded close. I glanced around and thought I saw her sitting at the kitchen table. I took a seat opposite and marvelled at the strength of my imagination. Apart from a mild cloudiness, it could have really been Mum sitting across from me.

'For what?' I asked.

Mum's face was free of the pain it had shown before she died. She appeared younger, happier. 'For pleading with you and begging you not to come here. For causing you so much doubt and pain.' Regret was clear in the tone of her voice.

All the way from my hometown in country Victoria, through central New South Wales and across the border into Queensland, Mum's entreaties had plagued my thoughts. Her begging had caused me a great deal of angst. But how did she know that?

I sighed and told her, 'I came because there's nothing for me in Sowees anymore. You're gone. Dad's gone. Not that that matters, I would never have stayed for him. Robert's also gone, for which I am strangely grateful.'

I paused, until the moment of saying it, I hadn't realised the relief I felt that we were no longer together.

'You were never suited love, but I knew you had to work that out for yourself.' Mum said gently.

'Yeah, well, it wasn't just not having Robert in my life,' I told her. 'My friends are married with children, *and* they all think I'm after their husbands. And to be honest, some of the husbands would be more than willing. Which is why I am no longer friends with *their* wives.'

Mum chuckled. It felt like old times. Except for the grandmother she had kept from me, there was very little we hadn't been able to talk about.

This wasn't the time to talk about why she hadn't told me her mother had been alive as I was growing up, or why she had never returned to her childhood home. I had already determined I wasn't going to spend the rest of my life running from Mum's fears.

She sighed, 'I know. I *am* sorry, Sandrine. I've been given this opportunity to tell you I was wrong to keep you from your destiny. This is what you were meant to do.

Destiny? Huh?

'Maybe,' I murmured.

Secretly, I doubted it. Mum's revelation had been driven by the foulness of terminal cancer. I shifted my mind back to the present, and the indistinct figure sitting across from me.

'Thank you for coming. I've missed talking to you. I've missed *you*,' I told her.

She looked at me fondly, 'You are so brave. I've missed you too, my dear. I am sorry, but I must go. I won't be back, but I know you will be okay now.'

'Goodbye, Mum. I love you,' I whispered.

With the fading of her image, a calmness settled over me. Any fragment of doubt, that I had done the right thing in coming to my grandmother's house, disappeared.

CHAPTER SEVEN

One afternoon a few weeks later, sitting on the back verandah, I watched the lengthening shadows of dusk, and couldn't remember the last time I'd felt so content.

Sipping on a glass of wine, I pondered over the sudden lack of electricity. A new fridge stood in place of my grandmother's older version, and since George informed me, on our first meeting, that the electricity here was unreliable, the wiring had been checked by an electrician.

Also on George's advice, if the electricity failed, I'd put water in the channel of an antique cooler standing in the shadiest section of the verandah. Hessian bags soaked up the water, and the breeze flowing around the verandah did the rest. It kept the butter, and a few other cold goods cool enough, though I wished the electricity had gone off at a decent hour. None of the electricians I phoned were available.

Before night could cast its dark velvet cloak across the land, I rose and lit the lamps I had found and cleaned, and which George had shown me how to work.

Even for autumn, the night seemed extra chilly. Coaxing the old, wood burning stove to life, I stood for a moment enjoying its warmth. For the first time since I arrived, I pondered the incongruity of the cool weather pattern on my grandmother's land, compared to the temperature on the other side of the gate. I didn't mull over it for long.

I cooked a meal on the gas stove I had bought and took it out to the back verandah to eat. Birds called to each other as they returned to their night-time roosts. The sun's descent to the horizon coloured the sky in shades of orange and red.

My peace shattered when heavy footsteps sounded on the front verandah.

Startled, I called, 'Who's there?'

No one answered.

Instantly, my sense of contentment vanished. Fear curled its fingers tightly around my bowels. For the first time, I was keenly aware of my isolation. Grabbing the knife from my empty plate, I crept around the verandah to the front.

A young man held onto the verandah rails for support. He swayed as if drunk, though I could not smell any alcohol. Blood, dried into dirty red and brown rivulets, streaked down his face. Glazed blue eyes shifted to meet mine.

'I need help,' he gasped.

'I can see that,' I told him, placing the knife on the verandah railing.

Putting my arm around him, I guided him into the now warm kitchen. He sat quietly while I bathed his head and face. A large cut on his head seemed to be the only wound he had, yet I felt something much more serious was wrong with him.

'I can't get back,' his tone held fear and anxiety.

'Back where?' I asked.

'Back. Just back. I'm not ready to go ...,' his voice trailed off.

He looked around as if searching for the place he was meant to go.

'I'm not sure,' he said. 'But I want to go back. Something's all wrong.'

'Wait here,' I instructed, before going to find my phone.

It was odd that I couldn't get a signal. I had used it only a couple of hours ago hoping to entice an electrician into some overtime.

Returning to the young man, I found him restless and muttering incoherently. Wiping his face with a cool cloth, I said, 'Can you tell me your name?'

The question and the sound of my voice appeared to calm his mind, for he answered clearly enough. 'John.'

'I'm Sandy. Come with me John,' I urged. 'You need to lie down, and I'll see if I can get some help.'

He struggled to his feet. I looped an arm around his waist to support him, and slowly we made our way into the spare bedroom.

Once on the bed, he reached out and grasped my hand, 'Don't leave me. Please don't leave me,' he begged. 'I don't want to go.'

I sat with him, held his hand, and wondered how I was going to get him help.

His body relaxed and he appeared to be asleep. I eased my hand from his grip, but he seemed to sense what I was doing, his eyes opened, and his grip tightened.

'Don't leave,' he pleaded.

'I need to get you some help,' I told him.

'No. I think it's too late. Don't leave. Please don't leave me. I've made a terrible mistake. It's Thea ... she told me she didn't love me anymore. As a boyfriend, I mean. She just wanted us to be friends, and I got angry, you see.'

I didn't, but I didn't tell him that. Instead, I held his hand until his breathing became slower and deeper. He seemed okay, but some innate sense filled me with foreboding - something strange was happening. I needed to get him to hospital.

I slid my phone from my pocket with my free hand and found the screen blank. It crossed my mind that maybe this was what George had been talking about when he told me to light a lantern if I needed help. What had he said - hang it on the verandah and he would come? I had to extricate myself from John first.

When John appeared asleep, I tried again to extract my hand, but any movement from me had him gripping hard and desperately, anchoring me to him.

'Don't go,' he murmured. 'Please don't go. Stay with me.'

Worried and feeling useless, I gave into his pleading and sat and watched him.

In the deepening silence, listening to his rhythmic breathing, weariness overtook me, I fell asleep holding his hand, and woke to him gently touching me on the shoulder. A calmness seemed to have overtaken him while he slept, and his eyes were clearer.

'I crashed the car,' his soft voice shadowed with a regret that showed in every line of his face. 'I did it deliberately, but I didn't mean for it to be so bad. I must have been going faster that I thought.'

The clouded look that entered his eyes told me he was lost in remembrance. I squeezed his hand in encouragement, letting him know - I was there. I was listening.

When he spoke again, John's voice was almost a whisper, 'I can't believe I've done something so incredibly stupid. I just meant to hit a small tree, but something in the grass flipped the car over. I wanted Anthea to feel sorry that she had rejected me. I thought that if I was hurt, she would realise what she had lost and come back to me. I thought I would regain her love, but now I realise how selfish and childish that was. Instead, I punished myself. Thea was right, she *has* outgrown me. Now, I'll never get the chance to say I'm sorry or have a ... a different life,' His voice broke, and tears ran unheeded down his cheeks.

I wanted to say, 'I'm sure there will be another opportunity,' but the words died before they reached my lips. I knew with a sickening certainty that there would not be another chance for him. Suddenly, I wasn't sure what to say. There was something else at play here, and deep inside of me a kernel of horror sprouted.

Had Mum told me the truth?

I shook my head trying to shake the thought out of my head.

No way!

There was no way John was dead. I was holding onto his hand, or least he was holding onto mine.

He was not dead!

But my heart beat a little faster, and my lungs seemed to have stopped working. The harder I tried to breathe, the more the air felt trapped in my chest. I opened my mouth and gulped air into my lungs.

Stay calm and stop being so bloody melodramatic. Oh course, he is not dead. We are sitting here having a conversation.

If John was aware of my panic, he gave no indication of it. His gaze had turned inwards, seeing something that I could not. He shook himself out of his reverie and turned to look at me.

'We were at school together. Thea was the popular girl, all the boys were interested in her, she could have taken her pick, but she chose me.'

John blinked away tears, sniffed and lay back on the pillows. His gaze traversed the ceiling, as if searching for answers that I thought would never come. After a moment, he appeared calmer, almost resigned. I had no idea what to say, so I said nothing. Somehow, I knew that my job was to listen.

'Will I be punished do you think?' He asked suddenly.

The question that popped into my head must have showed on my face, because he said, 'For killing myself, I mean.'

Killing himself? What the...?

I swallowed and asked as calmly as I could. 'Is that what you meant to do?'

I didn't really think he was dead, but he thought so, and I figured there was nothing I could do to dissuade him.

'No. I've been watching and reading too many silly stories. You must have seen or read them, you know someone gets hurt, and the one they love suddenly realise they love them after all. Pathetic, isn't it,' he said with a self-deprecating lopsided grin.

'No. I've seen and read a lot of stories like that myself. I just never believed them.'

'Clever you. Not me. I'm too stupid.'

'No, I'd rather think you're a romantic,' I told him. 'And I'm not clever, I thought the same thing until my father, whose attention I wanted more than anything, showed me I wasn't important to him.'

He looked at me then, fully for the first time. I could see that his focus had shifted from being totally absorbed with his own misery, to me.

'Oh God,' he whispered. 'I really have been so stupid, so self-absorbed, so ... so smug. If only I'd stopped to think instead, I was ....'

He didn't finish the sentence and eventually I changed the subject. 'I don't think you will be punished,' I said, trying to follow his previous line of thinking and reassure him. 'I think you've punished yourself enough. Anyway, I'm not sure I believe its punishment that awaits us on the other side.'

If indeed, it was the other side he was on or going to. On the edge of my mind, lingered the question – if he was on the other side then where was I? I veered rather quickly away from that somewhat terrifying thought.

I don't know why I was reassuring him, since I had no bloody idea, but it seemed to me to hold a truth, and whatever else I wanted to convey – it was the truth as I knew it, or as I sensed it.

'Thank you for staying with me. I'm glad you're here.' His voice trailed off.

For a while, we sat together without words. Our breathing synchronised as an unexpected peacefulness settled over us.

Suddenly he was alert, as if listening to something I couldn't hear.

'I don't think it will be long now. I can sense them getting closer. I think they have given me this time with you so that I could ...,' He paused, and a slow, lopsided, grin touched his lips. 'Adjust ... I think that's the right word, but it's a hell of an adjustment.'

John squeezed my hand and released it. His eyes closed and his face relaxed, smoothing out all the creases that his anxiety had wrought. He looked very young and very vulnerable. My heart ached for him, and sudden tears stung my eyes.

I sat and watched him and wondered why he was so convinced he was dead.

He can't be dead!

This thought had barely entered my mind when a tiny gleam of light emanated from his body. I blinked several times and rubbed my eyes. I was overtired. Was I hallucinating?

As the light within John grew, another more colourful and much brighter light entered the room, and with it, I gained the sense of another presence.

With a growing sense of awe combined with a hard knot of fear, I watched as the two lights merged then abruptly blinked out.

I was left, sitting alone in a darkened room with a mind gone suddenly blank, unable to comprehend what I had witnessed.

The bed where John had lain not a moment before, was empty.

CHAPTER EIGHT

I woke with a start the following morning. The bright light shining through the curtains told me the sun was well up. Automatically, I reached for my phone to check the time. The screen showed eight o'clock.

Slowly, I became aware that I was fully dressed. For several moments, I lay trying to process why I wasn't in my pyjamas. Little by little, the previous night unfolded in my consciousness, and John's face appeared in my mind.

Had I dreamt John and the light? It seemed so real.

I sprang from my bed and moved swiftly across the hall into the spare room.

The bed had obviously been used. The sheets were soiled and blood-stained cloths lay in a bowl on the bedside table. With my increasing sense of incredulity, my heart rate flared so strongly I could feel a pulse, that threatened to choke me, in my throat. Bewilderment closed my mind. I couldn't think – I could barely breathe; I lowered myself into the chair beside the bed and stared at it.

John had been convinced he was dead, but he'd seemed so very much alive. I sat beside the empty bed with part of my mind full of random thoughts:

I held his hand.
We had spoken.
I cleaned his blood.
It hadn't been a dream.

Another section of my mind was blank with incomprehension; how long I sat there with a tug of war going on inside my head, I couldn't say. The sun was well up in the sky, I estimated it was mid-morning or after when I stood and began walking aimlessly about the house, picking things up and putting them down again.

From the verandah, I stared in the direction of George's place.

He said to contact him, did he mean it?

I don't even know the man.

What would I say to him?

Dismissing any thought of contacting him, I descended the steps. Kicking off my shoes, I stood barefoot on the ground, staying there until I felt connected to the earth.

Gradually, the peace of nature eased its way into my being. A cool breeze fanned my face, lifting my hair as if gentle fingers were caressing my head. The anxiety, that had been plaguing me all morning, slowly dissipated and my breathing settled into an even rhythm.

Slipping my feet back into my shoes, I made my way to the orchard, where I picked an orange and sat on the log under the macadamia tree.

Midway through removing the orange peel, my mind abruptly shifted and once again, I saw Mum and recalled her words, '*It's a doorway for the dead. I found it terrifying as I child. I think I could see them more clearly than Mum. She saw only the newly dead, but I could see the ones that came for them.*'

Words that I'd dismissed as being the result of drugs and profound illness.

A slight rustle in the grass brought me back from the memory of Mum. George was standing a few feet away, watching me. His eyes assessed me; to avoid them I glanced down at the orange in my hand and began peeling it again. When I finished, I returned my gaze to George's face and saw concern in his eyes.

Deliberately, I placed an orange segment in my mouth and shifted my gaze to somewhere past his shoulder. Sweet juice filled my mouth, it switched my attention to chewing and savouring, allowing only physical sensations to occupy my mind.

Not put off by my behaviour. 'Did you have a visitor last night?' George asked. His voice was quiet, gentle, as if talking to someone very ill.

I nodded without looking at him. From the corner of my eye, I watched his approach. He picked each foot up and put it down again with a deliberateness that looked like he was navigating his way through a mine field. His hand held his mobile phone; when he was standing in front of me, he lifted the screen up to my face.

'Is this him?'

I sat and chewed and ignored the hand in front of my face.

George's patience outlasted me until John's face looked back at me from the screen. A younger, happier man then the one I encountered last night.

I nodded again and muttered a soft, 'Yes.'

'They found his car and his body this morning.' George informed me.

'Oh god, it's true,' I whimpered softly. And burst into tears.

Lifting me from the log, George gathered me into his arms. Large, warm, and very much alive, he held me while I sobbed out my grief, disbelief, and the many other unidentifiable and conflicting emotions that coursed through me.

When my sobs subsided, he murmured into my hair, 'Have you eaten?'

I nodded my head.

'Other than the orange?'

I shook my head, wordlessly.

'Come,' he said, taking my hand and leading me toward the house.

I sat on the verandah, guarding the stillness in my mind so that random thoughts could not enter and disturb my peace.

In the kitchen, George noisily opened and closed cupboards, finding his way around.

He emerged eventually with two plates of bacon and eggs as well as coffee, toast and an assortment of jam, honey, and vegemite. Breakfast had become lunch, and I found I was hungry after all. We ate, silence settled around and in us, and the first links of a profound bond were formed, but not yet acknowledged.

I was somewhere deep inside my mind when George touched my shoulder bringing me back to the present. My gaze fell to the table which had been cleared of the breakfast dishes. I glanced around and up at George.

'Sorry,' I said, but what I was sorry for I couldn't have said. Not being present, I guessed. Time had passed without me being aware.

'I've cleaned up,' he told me. 'I'll go unless you want to talk. Have you got any questions?'

He sat across the table from me, his dark eyes filled with something I couldn't categorise, as well as kindness and understanding.

'He was real.' I insisted. 'He bled. He talked to me. How could they have found his body when he was with me? I have the proof in the blood-stained cloths, the unmade bed ... it doesn't make sense.'

'Did you see him go, by any chance?' He asked softly.

'Huh? Well yes. No, not exactly. There was a light and ... some sort of presence in the room. I feel like I'm going mad!' I exclaimed suddenly. 'It just doesn't make sense.'

I seemed to be repeating myself.

'Don't try to 'make sense' of it,' George said, making air quotes with his fingers. 'Believe me, this doesn't fit anyone's world view; it just is. You'll drive yourself crazy trying to make it adapt to how you believe the world should be.'

I looked at him without really seeing him, his words washed over me. I understood what he was saying, but it held no meaning. I retreated then to somewhere inside myself – into a void of quietness, where I felt enclosed by a bubble of peace.

I felt George leave rather than saw him go. I was alone in the void without thought, giving my subconscious mind and my soul space to untangle and recover.

CHAPTER NINE

A loud caw nearby brought me back from the calming emptiness into which I had gone to shelter. I blinked several times and became aware of filtered sunlight touching my face. A cool breeze eddied around me. I turned my head sightly to find the owner of the loud voice sitting on the verandah railing not far from me. With its bright, intelligent eyes, the raven watched me for several heartbeats before flying away.

Reality washed over me, I stood, took several deep breaths, and needing something to do, I went to restore order to the spare bedroom.

No wonder Mum didn't want me to come here.

That small nagging voice in the back of my mind stayed with me. I spent the rest of the day thinking not only about John, but of Mum as a child, surrounded by the dead. What had life been like for a child, living in a house where death was a constant visitor?

George came to see me a week later. 'The funeral is tomorrow. At two. I'll pick you up.'

The thought of a funeral never crossed my mind. I had seen John leave, and putting his body in the ground seemed to be superfluous. His family needed to say goodbye, not me.

'Why are you telling me? I wasn't planning to go.'

'Because the townsfolk need to see you. By going to the funeral, they will know that you guided John on his way to the other side.'

I stared at him in consternation for several seconds before asking, 'Is that what my grandmother used to do?' Not bothering to keep the disbelief from my voice.

'Yes. She attended the funerals of all the sudden deaths in the area. Or at least, the ones who came to her, most did, and if they did, she attended the funeral so that the families would know. John's family are part of the original settlers. They will gain comfort from knowing that you'll continue the tradition. It is important to the ones that know or believe anyway. The newcomers to the town believe it to be superstition.'

'If you're sure,' I told him, doubtfully.

The church was full of mourners when George and I arrived. We found a seat in the back. People sitting close turned their heads to stare at me for several seconds, before nudging each other and turning away. George took my hand and held it throughout the ceremony and the graveside. Grateful for the comfort his large body provided, I remained attached to his side.

Curiosity filled people's faces. Since it was such a small community, I guessed they were trying to place me. Several nodded at George, but their glances at me held various messages. Some curious, some interested, some fearful.

Do they know?

'What's going on, George?' I whispered.

His only response was to give my hand a reassuring squeeze.

After the ceremony, as people began to drift away, I heard talk of attending a wake. George didn't move, I took his hold on my hand as a signal to be still.

My attention wandered to a distraught young woman being comforted by a man; I wondered if she was the love that John had lost, when George squeezed my hand again.

A man stood in front of us, I saw at once that he was an older version of John. He must have caught the recognition in my eyes because fresh tears flowed down his face. A woman, his wife I gathered by her propriety hold on his arm, gazed at me with cold eyes from a face ravaged by grief.

'Come away Brett,' she urged pulling on his arm.

'You have my deepest condolences,' I told them. 'I know what it's like to lose someone you love very much.'

Brett resisted her grasp on his arm and stared intently at me for several heartbeats.

'You saw him then? He came to you?'

My first thought was, how could he possibly have known that?

A slight squeeze on my hand from George told me all I needed to know.

'Yes,' I said softly.

'Thank God. Oh, Thank God. He passed in the light then?'

I didn't understand the question and it must have shown on my face.

'My wife and I,' he paused and took hold of the hand pulling at his arm. 'We were told it looked like he had driven off the road deliberately. That he had ...,' he gulped, 'taken his own life. We weren't sure if ....' His voice, filled with pain and anguish, fell to a whisper.

I cleared my throat, 'It was an accident,' I told them.

'How can you know that with any certainty?' John's mother snapped.

'I ...,' Suddenly, I was unsure how to explain.

'You know how she knows, Jill.' George's quiet, deep voice challenged her.

'He ... his girlfriend had just broken up with him,' I said in a rush.

'How ...?'

'Let her finish,' George intoned.

'John thought that if he had a slight accident then maybe she would realise that she still loved him. He misjudged where he went off the road. The car flipped. I promise, he didn't mean to kill himself. Towards the end, I mean before he passed over, he realised that she was right, that she had outgrown him. I'm deeply sorry. He was a lovely, caring young man who made a mistake.'

Brett's wife clutched at her throat, 'Oh, My God, Oh My God. What they say is true, you *do* see the dead. I didn't believe my mother-in-law when she told me. I thought it was an old wives tale.'

Her blue eyes, once full of cold hostility, softened as she reached out her hand. I took it gently in my own. 'Thank you. Thank you so much,' she said earnestly.

Her husband wrapped his arm around her shoulders, gently drawing her away. She was still looking back at me as they left.

Another group, women my mother's age, waited in the background. As John's parents moved on, they moved forwards. Surprisingly, Beatrice Milledge was at their forefront and as she drew close, she placed a basket in my arms.

'We came hoping to see you today, Sandrine. Your presence here today tells us that the gift of the Legg women to this community, will live on. We know now that those who are taken from us too soon, will continue to be loved and guided towards the light. This is a welcome gift from everyone here. Please accept it with our deepest gratitude.'

'I ... I ...,' the words refused to come. Even as the basket rested in my hands, George took it from me without a word, and I was surrounded by women who took turns to gather me in their arms.

One said, 'Most of the young don't realise the spiritual world is as real as the phones they hold in their hands. But we are working to educate them.'

Many of the women whispered as they hugged me, 'Bless you for the work you do.'

'Thank you for coming,' said another.

As their words filtered deep into my soul, a profound sense of belonging enveloped me. I watched them walk away, knowing that they had come to perform a blessing and welcome me home.

CHAPTER TEN

We were quiet on the way home. My mind was full of thoughts of Mum and the kind of life she had endured with Dad. Her life with him had been a kind of hell, yet she had stayed with him instead of returning to her childhood home and her mother's support. Now that I had experienced John's transition and the love and support of the community, it was difficult to understand what had driven her away.

Fear perhaps? Her youth maybe?

What was here, wasn't so terrifying as to make her stay away for so long, or to disown her own mother. And certainly not to put up with Dad for so long. I was having a great deal of difficulty understanding her choices.

Occasionally, I felt George's gaze on me, though he held his silence and seemed content to let me brood.

At home, he dropped me off at the gate. I was thankful to be alone with my contemplations. A part of me wished Mum had told me about the house being a portal for the dead before she became ill. I might not have blamed the drugs and the illness and listened to her. Or not. No-one with a rational mind would believe what I had experienced.

Before I alighted from the car, George handed me an envelope.

'Vivienne left this for you. She said to give it to you if I thought you would stay.'

Barely glancing at the letter, I shoved it to the bottom of my handbag, waved to George as he drove off and turned away. Whatever my grandmother had to say, it would keep for another day. I had enough to think about.

I was shutting the gate when, out of the corner of my eye, movement caught my attention.

The same old man who had given me directions to the house, was walking towards me. I waited, warily watching his approach.

He didn't look any different to when I had first seen him. He appeared to be wearing exactly the same set of clothes, only this time I noticed his pants were held up by a thin piece of rope instead of a belt. The felt hat on his head had definitely seen better days; it looked like the hats I had seen in photographs from another age. The stem of a pipe protruded above his shirt pocket. I hadn't noticed that the other day either. There was a calmness of the bush about him; though I had the distinct impression, that, like the bush, he could turn dangerous in a heartbeat.

What was his role in this?

Stopping on the other side of the gate, he removed the pipe from his pocket and began to tap it gently on the gate to displace the old tobacco. He didn't acknowledge me; it was as if I didn't exist.

Curiosity got the better of me. I stayed and watched as he took out a battered old tin from his pant pocket and calmly began to tamp tobacco into the bowl of his pipe. He sucked on it a couple of times and when he was satisfied, lit the pipe, and took a few tentative puffs. Coils of smoke rose lazily and disappeared. Taking one last draw on the pipe, the old man removed it from between his teeth.

'You've decided to stay then I see,' he said.

Obviously, he was not interested in social niceties if that was his greeting.

'How do you figure that since I haven't actually decided yet?'

'The house,' he indicated it with a nod of his head.

I turned and gasped. The house shone. The shadows, that had surrounded it when I arrived, were gone.

It looks like it's come to life!

'OH! I ... well, that's strange,' was all I could think to say. My eyes must have been playing tricks the day I first saw it.

The old man smirked. There was something very annoying about that knowing grin. I felt like hitting him. Maybe that would wipe the smile from his face. The pipe was back in between his teeth, mischievous brown eyes held a smile that made me feel as if I was being laughed at.

If there was a joke, I couldn't see it.

'George told me your name is Rupert. My name is Sandrine, Sandy.' I told him, tartly.

'I know your name, and since you're going to stay, get George to bring around some hens and a cow and calf. Vivienne used the milk and eggs to barter for meat and things she couldn't grow herself. I expect you'll do the same.'

The events of the day caught up with me, I was tired and cranky, and I found this strange old man annoying. It was hard to keep the bite out of my tone.

'Well, you expect wrong,' I informed him. 'I have no need to barter for anything, I can go to the supermarket.'

Apart from the money, I'd inherited from Vivienne, Mum had left me with enough money to live on for the rest of my life. The only part Dad had let her play in his life was to look after the finances. She had, unbeknown to me, been a wiz at investing. After Mum's death, I inherited everything, though I didn't see any need to share that knowledge with Rupert.

I had no intention of bartering. And getting a cow! Was he mad?

'You may think you won't need to barter, but some of your guests will stay longer than your last one,' he informed me. 'Not all wish to pass on so quickly.'

What the hell!

'Guests! Do you mean John? How do you know about ...?' I stopped, glared at him, 'Stay longer? What is that supposed to mean?'

Rupert puffed on his pipe, watching me without answering any of the questions that tumbled from my lips. The message on his face was clear – can't you understand plain English? He obviously wasn't going to answer, so I changed the subject.

'If you knew my grandmother's name was Vivienne, why did you call this Violet's place the other day?'

'Because she was the first, wasn't she.' It was more statement than question, but I heard the query and did not understand it.

'The first what?' I was beginning to think the old man's elevator didn't go all the way to the top.

Silence, and a few more puffs on the pipe before he finally spoke.

'Custodian or guardian, you can give her any name you like. She came with the first ship, and her legacy is passed from mother to daughter. Vera was the first to refuse but Vivienne knew you would come. She always said you would and here you are.' His keen eyes assessed me with a knowingness that disconcerted me.

'Aren't you?' He insisted.

I returned his gaze and answered him with another question. 'You speak as if you knew my mother. Do you know why she left?' I told him.

'I knew them all.' He said enigmatically.

'That's impossible,' I snapped. 'The first ship was two hundred years ago.'

He grinned around the pipe clamped between his teeth, then with a long-suffering expression removed it, 'You witness a transition from this life to the next, then tell me something is impossible?'

I took a deep breath, released it slowly and wished with all my heart that I had listened to Mum.

What have I gotten myself into?

'You said you knew my mother? She never told me about this place. Do you know why she left and why she never returned? I think it was because she was very frightened, and she didn't want me to come.'

He studied in me silence then said, 'Vera saw more than most. She was very young and frightened, and Vivienne didn't understand her talents. If I'm right, you will have the same abilities. Violet was the most powerful guardian I have ever seen, but I believe that power was weakened by the men they choose as fathers for their offspring.'

'You make it sound as if they didn't have husbands but chose a … a sperm donor.' I told him, confused at the way he'd phrased the statement.

'If you mean by 'sperm donor', joining with a man in order to beget a child, then you're right. None married and they chose who would father their child. Most choose wisely but not all. Vivienne made the wisest choice; pity her other choices weren't so wise.'

'You knew my grandfather?'

'I did. Interesting man. In a small way, he also had the gift. It's a pity he didn't stay; he may have been able to help Vera.'

'Why didn't he stay? Is he still alive?'

Rupert put the pipe back into his mouth and puffed on it for several long annoying moments, before he deigned to remove it and answer me.

'Long gone. And I don't know why he didn't stay, that was between him and Vivienne.'

I studied him in silence then asked, 'How can George see you? Especially, if as you say, you have 'known them all'. You must be a ghost too.' It was hard to keep the scepticism from my voice.

A smile touched his eyes, 'You don't believe me now. But you will. George sees me because I allow it, and because he too has a passing amount of the gift.'

'What's a passing amount?'

Rupert shrugged, 'You have enough to think about for now. One day, we'll sit down and talk if you want, but not today,'

'I'm not sure I *am* going to stay, but if I do, I can't see why I would need livestock. I wouldn't know what to buy anyway.'

'You will need a cow and chickens, and I suggest you get that garden going. Any visitor that you have, cannot be left alone. I told Vivienne that I would look after you if and when you came; therefore, I will. Get George to help you,' he said emphatically.

He seemed so sure; a tiny seed of doubt planted itself in my mind. I wouldn't know what to do with a cow. And a garden! How ridiculous! That, I would never do.

For several seconds, the silence lay heavy between us, with him puffing on his pipe and me glaring at him before he continued.

'Also, none of your modern things are going to work when you have a visitor, and don't bother trying to get anyone in to fix it, they won't be able to find the place, it is sealed during the transition. And if you get a cat, it won't eat the mice.'

He turned and walked away.

My mouth had fallen open with his pronouncements, I closed my mouth with a snap.

Infuriating old fool. How could he have known I was thinking of getting a cat? Though it doesn't take much to figure out there would be mice in the house. Not only would I get a cat, but I would also get a dog, to guard against crazy old men!

CHAPTER ELEVEN

A few days after my meeting with Rupert, even though I had not had any contact with him, George appeared with a lovely cream coloured cow. I fell in love with her immediately.

'She's a Jersey,' he informed me. 'They give good creamy milk and have placid natures. We have time to restore the bails before the calf is born, then she'll give you plenty of milk if you need it.'

'Have you been speaking to Rupert?'

He grinned. 'He may have stopped by.'

'He seems to think he is dead,' I told George, who just nodded.

Remembering John, I refrained from telling him how crazy that was and asked. 'Do you believe his bizarre tales?'

'I don't just believe. I know he is who he says he is, and that he has been assisting the guardians ever since they came to Australia. I don't know what his connection was to Violet, but it was strong, and he has been here ever since, watching over all her descendants. This place is known as Violet's Place, has he told you that?

Surreptitiously, I pinched myself. No, definitely awake. Just listening to a seemingly perfectly ordinary man giving a logical explanation for the weird, wonderful and if it hadn't been for John, the unbelievable.

'Humph,' was all I was able to manage to say, and hoped he took it as an agreement.

I took a deep breath, shook my head to clear it then turned to the sweet creature standing before me. Approaching her cautiously, I held out my hand for her to sniff. Her large gentle eyes regarded me curiously, before she slowly stretched out her long neck to touch my hand with her nose.

Growing bold at her acceptance of me, I moved closer and scratched her gently behind the ears. Her eyes closed, and she bent her head to give my nails greater access.

George laughed, 'You've got the knack. I think you two will get along very well together.'

After I helped George repair the ancient though solid bails, he taught me how to use them.

Coaxing Lavender, (as I decided to call the cow) into the bails, he showed me how to leg rope her. A little bit of molasses kept her quiet while I handled her teats in preparation for the day when I really would have to milk her. I wasn't looking forward to that day and hoped all my 'visitors', as Rupert called them, were ready to pass on as quickly as John.

One morning, I woke to find George in the back yard, with the chook pen restored and six hens clucking contentedly on the ground at his feet. I made breakfast and after we had eaten, we sat together in contented silence. I was amazed by his ability to sit in silence with me and not feel any awkwardness between us. I couldn't help comparing him to Robert, who I realised now, had been uncomfortable with silence.

After George left, I dug the letter my grandmother had written from my handbag and sat on the back deck. It rested on the table before me for several minutes, with me gazing at it and wondering what can of worms I would be opening. I wasn't convinced I had made the right decision to stay, but the thought of leaving felt worse. Taking a deep breath, I reached for the letter.

My darling Sandrine

May I call you Sandy. Sandrine is such a mouthful, and it is a shame Vera deviated from the family tradition of using first names beginning with 'V'. It seems we were never destined to meet, and you have so much to learn. And you must be interested in learning and going to stay, or you would not be reading this letter. I was very firm with George; he was not to give you the letter unless he thought you were going to stay. What we do, our family of women, and it is always women, it's an apprenticeship really and cannot be taught with a single letter. I had always hoped Vera would return once she matured. I can only imagine the fear in her was too great, which to my sorrow, I did not recognise until it was too late. I was fortunate to have a mother and a grandmother to guide me, but they had passed on by the time Vera arrived, thus I raised Vera alone. Very difficult under any circumstances, but especially these. Had she come back, we could have all been together. A dear wish of mine. I have no doubt Harriet Gould will fill you in on my failings as a mother. She is a very dear friend and correct in her assessments. Anyway, enough of that, water under the bridge. Never dwell on the past, once it is gone, it is gone and can never be recovered. There is only now. And now you are reading my letter, I do not know what to tell you. There is so much you will experience, and it will all be different. The most important thing to remember is that the ones who come to us have been torn from their bodies suddenly, and unlike those who face death after a long illness, have not had time to adjust. And more often than not they have no idea that they are what is known as 'dead' and are in fact in a state of transition. Dead to this world perhaps but not dead in that they no longer exist. Depending on how deep their denial, some will still bleed, some will even eat, the main thing is to allow them time to adjust and treat them as guests, and as much as you would like to hurry the process sometimes, it cannot be done. (Remember, being 'dead' doesn't make one's spirit pleasant, cooperative, or even decent.) Rupert will help with the spirit world though sometimes he forgets himself and gives advice on the temporal world. George will help you with corporeal matters. There is so much I would like to tell you. At times you may be scared, though I think the main thing to remember is that you are protected, and no harm will come to you. And always remember, You are in charge. Never let the ones who come forget that. And if needed you can call on the beings of light for aid. They will come (if they deem it necessary) but they will not force the transition. For your own peace of mind, if necessity deems it, the guests can be asked to leave the property. You may see some of the ones who still roam the earth, be wary of the those who I have refused, they may come to you. There are so many different circumstances, I cannot possibly explain them all in one single letter. If you need help at all, no matter what form of help is needed, hang a lantern on the side verandah facing George's place. He will come. George is reliable and trustworthy. Rupert will hear you if you call. He may come. Usually. Sometimes. Thank you for continuing our tradition of helping with the transition, it is more important in today's world than ever. We have lost touch with the acceptance of dying, for it is only in the knowledge of dying that we may learn to live.

With fondest regards and all my best wishes,

Your Grandmother,

Vivienne.

After reading the letter several times over, my heart beat faster and the only coherent and recurring thought in my mind was - *What the hell had I gotten myself into.*

Despite losing both my parents, like most people, I never truly considered life as a precious gift or death as being close and present with every breath I took. If my experience with John was anything to go by, then I was going to be constantly reminded that death was no longer something that I could consider as a future possibility, it was now and in every waking moment.

The sun had set by the time I gathered up the letter and placed it in an old tin I'd found amongst Vivienne's belongings. A part of me wondered why I hadn't packed my bags and run screaming from the place. Another deeper part knew that it was because, for some inexplicable reason, I felt at home and that this was where I was meant to be.

Maybe George and Rupert weren't the only crazy ones?

CHAPTER TWELVE

The sun had barely peeked over the horizon and a light fog hovered close to the earth one morning when, feeling restless, I set out to explore the twenty acres Grandmother Vivienne had bequeathed to me.

For a time, I walked the fence line, then set off across country toward a grove of trees. The land was not flat as I first thought, it had been an optical illusion. The terrain sloped gently downwards to the edge of a rather deep gully; through which, a stream of cool and inviting water flowed.

I scrambled down the steep embankment to the floor of the small valley and sat on the creek bank watching the shallow water ripple over rocks and sand.

Removing my shoes, I stepped into the icy water and gasped. I hadn't expected it to be quite so freezing or so painful, my feet felt like they were on fire.

Resisting my first instinct to jump out of the glacial water, I forced myself to keep moving. As my body adjusted and the pain receded, I found joy in the feel of the gritty sand between my toes. Small fish flit from rock to boulder to evade the invader of their territory. When the depth of the water grew too deep to wade, I moved to the embankment and replaced my shoes.

A track along the creek edge led to a bridge where a fast-moving current flowed into a deep pool of water before surging onwards to its distant destination.

It was the bridge, I realised, I had driven over many times when I had searched for the entrance to the property. I needed to look at a map, but I was convinced that the small valley and creek served as an unfenced boundary to the land I now owned.

Coffee! The sudden desire caught me by surprise. Why hadn't I bought a flask of coffee with me. The glass of water I sculled before leaving on my morning adventure was a poor substitute for the coffee

I now craved. A picnic breakfast would have been heaven, if only I had thought of it.

Despite craving coffee, the air was sweet and pure, and peace settled around me like a soft cloak. Notwithstanding my recent, startling, and strange visitor, I was suddenly glad that I had moved to this beautiful property.

On the road above, a vehicle approached slowly. My first thought was another early morning enthusiast, enjoying the peace of the dawn, and watching the world come slowly to life.

Overhead, in the middle of the bridge, the car stopped. A bag flew over the side hitting the water with a loud splat. The car then sped away.

Shit! Something's in the bag. Oh My God!

I was in the water, (somehow without my shoes), with horror and the sudden shock of freezing water pumping adrenaline into my veins. In seconds, I arrived at the bag's entry point and dived to the bottom of the creek.

A powerful undercurrent had already moved the sack. I swam to the surface, released the stale air from my lungs, pulled fresh oxygen in, and dived again, angling crossways this time.

Despite the apparent clearness of the surface water, it was difficult to see anything on the murky creek bed. Dimly, I spotted the bag being dragged, by the current, along the bottom of the creek. My lungs felt like they were about to burst. I couldn't risk a second rise to the surface to take another fresh breath; I would lose the sack, and its occupant would die a horrible death. Determination drove me forward until a desperate, hooking motion with one finger snagged the bag, thereby stopping its impetus. With much fumbling, I seized a firmer hold.

Relief, and a resolve to save us both, flooded through me. As my feet touched the bottom of the creek bed, I gave a forceful thrust, propelling us to the surface.

Out of breath and energy and struggling to keep the hessian sack above the water line, we flowed downstream with the current.

When I *could* talk, I said, 'You still alive, in there?'

The sound of my voice stirred the occupant of the bag, it gave a weak mewl, and I knew the cat I'd saved was still alive and more importantly, fighting.

Navigating my way to the water's edge, I said 'Sorry mate,' as I half pushed, and half threw the bag onto the creek bank. With a lot of grunting, pushing, and pulling, I slowly heaved myself onto the bank and lay exhausted, beside the bag.

'You better appreciate this, whoever you are,' I groaned. 'Instead of jumping into a freezing, bloody creek, I could have found a better way of getting a cat. I nearly killed myself for you.'

The prisoner growled, no doubt he wanted out, but I was too bloody tired to even think about releasing him or her.

CHAPTER THIRTEEN

Outside, the day hovered on the edge of sliding into the night. Shadows lengthened, and a cool breeze had replaced the warmth of the sun. The grumble in my belly urged me to think about food, but I wanted to finish the chapter I was reading. For reasons I never examined, I hadn't installed a television and found I didn't miss having one. George left his old newspapers in my letter box; I retrieved them and kept up with worldly events. Books, magazines, jigsaw puzzles and games on my phone kept me occupied when I ran out of jobs to do, which come to think of it was never. When I had had enough of work, I simply stopped and amused myself in other ways.

I switched on a light and before returning to my book, glanced at the cat. His position had not changed. From his bed beside the warm stove, through slitted lids, his green eyes watched me as he so often had during the two months of his convalescence.

Every day since I'd saved him, I wondered why I had, without any thought, thrown myself into the deep waters of a freezing creek to save an unknown animal.

I could have died!

Even now, occasionally I had flashbacks of struggling to breathe and feeling too weak to swim. Obviously, I needed my head examined. I mean who does that? I figured I had been temporarily insane.

Chance, as I'd named him, showed no sign of gratitude. Though why would I expect anything from a cat, especially one who appeared to have been wild before I had dragged him from the creek and into my life.

His youth was not far behind him, two years old the vet thought. Chance was large, with a small tuft of white in the centre of his forehead, providing a spot of interest in an otherwise ebony black coat. He was also fiercely independent. If he hadn't been so weak from being nearly drowned and from loss of blood caused by the other wounds to his body, which according to the vet, appeared to have been made with a knife, he would have fled the moment I opened the bag.

Antibiotics cleared away all the bacteria from his lungs and his wounds; the regrowth of his fur where it had been shaved, the only sign he'd had any wounds at all.

I'd been sure that once his wounds *had* healed, Chance would leave, never to return. Instead, he graciously allowed me to provide him with food, water, and a warm bed. My reward was, apparently, his not so friendly company and him staring at me like I had two heads.

A rumbling growl from Chance lifted my head from the book, and I glanced at him in surprise. His silence was the only trait I truly appreciated about my new housemate. His tail flicked slowly from side to side. Chance had moved from relaxed and half asleep to a hunting crouch. His eyes, now round and wide, stared intently at the back door which stood open to the night air. The growl deepened from a warning to something more menacing.

I placed the book on the table, moved to the door and peered out into the shadowy twilight. Chance stalked before me, as if he were my protector.

The dim light hid more than it revealed. I stared out into the gloom wondering what the cat sensed that I could not. Beside me, Chance's growl deepened, and a quick glance down at him revealed an animal ready to attack.

But what?

Since there was nothing obvious close to the house, I focused my search outwards and allowed my gaze to roam further away. Out of the corner of my eye, a slight movement caught my attention.

About fifteen metres from the steps, stood a wraithlike figure. There was a hazy opaqueness to her that made the hairs on the back of my neck stand to attention. A cold shiver slid down my spine.

She floated towards the house.

My breath caught with a gasp, suspended somewhere deep inside my chest, I struggled to move air in or out of my lungs.

When she was ten metres away, I could see the expression on her face more clearly. My heartbeat soared up into my throat so rapidly I felt like my airway had closed. Chance's tail beat across my ankles with a fast and angry rhythm. His growling never ceased, which I not only found comforting, but it also helped me to find my voice.

'You are forbidden to come any closer.' I squeaked out.

What made me say that I had no idea, but it stopped her advance, and a sly grin slithered across her lips.

For several moments we watched each other; in that time my pulse slowed to a more normal rhythm, and air eased its way slowly in and out of my lungs. As the seconds slipped by, I came to the certain realisation that she was not among the newly dead.

Chance's attitude never changed - he was on guard, ready to attack at any moment.

Nothing in my grandmother's letter had prepared me for this, or was this woman one of ones she said roamed the earth? I quickly sifted several options through my mind of what to do next and came up with nothing. I decided simple was best, so I said, 'How can I help you?'

Apparently unprepared for the question, consternation replaced the sneer on her face. It seemed she had not only recognised but enjoyed the fear that had flooded through me when I first saw her. Now that fear was gone, or at least appeared to anyway, she was no longer sure of herself.

'I am sure if you call, they will come,' I told her.

Meaning the beings of light who had come for John. At least I hoped they would. Did she know who I meant?

It seemed she did, fury flashed across her face. 'I will never call. I will not leave this life.

Life! The bloody woman was dead, didn't she realise! Well, they say perception is everything.

I didn't disabuse her of the notion that she was no longer alive, (or at least no longer inhabited an earthly body), but I wanted her as far away from me as she could possibly go. It was clear she was trouble.

'Your choice,' I told her. 'But you are not welcome here. You must leave.'

'I go where I please,' she informed me.

'No, you don't,' I replied firmly. 'You do not have permission to enter this house, and you can only come back here again if you seek the help of those who aide in the transition.'

'How is it you know so much? You are new here, this I know.'

'Call it instinct,' I told her. Or dumb luck I silently added.

'I see you have a familiar,' she stated, indicating Chance. Are you a witch?'

A familiar? What century was she born in?

'He is a cat.' I told her emphatically. 'Not a demon.'

At least, I hoped he wasn't. A quick downward glimpse revealed an animal who looked demonic in his ferociousness.

The look she spread between Chance and I said she clearly didn't believe me.

'Even if you not know it Witch, he *is* your familiar, and will do your bidding,' the sneer had returned to her face and voice. After a long interval of studying me, she added, '*If* you can learn to talk with him ... and control him.'

Her image became clearer as she talked; her attire, which consisted of a long skirt and a long-sleeved blouse, appeared reminiscent of another era.

'What is your name?' I asked.

'My name is my own and not for you to know,' she couldn't keep the scorn from her voice.

As much as I wanted to see her gone, curiosity overcame me. 'How long have you been wandering the earth?'

'Too long, Witch,' she replied with yet another non-answer.

A predatory look or something similar, flicked across her eyes and was gone so quickly, I wondered for a moment if I had been mistaken.

Chance's tail beat faster on my ankles. Was it a warning?

I stepped back. 'Leave. You are not welcome,' I said firmly.

She gave a tight smile that didn't reach her eyes. 'So, you do talk with each other, even if *you* don't know it yet,' she repeated her cryptic nonsense.

With that mysterious response she faded, until there was only a misty outline of her against the backdrop of a dark night that had crept in without me being aware.

On high alert, Chance and I stayed on the verandah long after the wraith had left. The air was cold and full of menace. I wrapped my arms around myself. It took some time before a modicum of peace eased its way into my centre. I released my grip, allowing my arms to settle at my side.

As if that had been a signal, Chance sat and licked his paws, then with one last glance into the black night, he turned, tail erect and strolled through the back door.

I shivered involuntarily, followed Chance in and shut the door firmly behind me. I had questions I needed to put to Rupert, but they could wait until morning.

Hunger had caught up with me.

CHAPTER FOURTEEN

Rupert was waiting for me on the back verandah the following morning, when I opened the door. Restless and vigilant, I had delayed going to bed, so woke much later than I normally would.

Chance, for the first time since he arrived, slept on my bed that night. A soft growl from him roused me briefly at daybreak. He settled quickly, and sleep swiftly reclaimed me.

Sleepily, I stared at Rupert before retreating into the kitchen to make coffee.

Sipping my coffee, I recounted the events of the previous evening. Rupert sat and listened without saying a word or even acknowledging that I was speaking. Was he deaf? Not interested? Couldn't he even show a scrap of concern?

When I finished speaking, we sat in silence.

Silence! The last thing I expected.

'How did you come by the cat?'

The cat! A scary wraith had visited me, and he was interested in the cat!

He showed more interest when I told him how I had rescued Chance from drowning.

He nodded. 'You have done well. While the cat is here, it is unlikely she will bother you again. Be on guard when visitors come, she will try to entice them to join her. She is one of the lost ones. Dardanelle is her name; she was a wanderer in Violet's time and refuses help. Continue to forbid her. She brings trouble.'

With that, Rupert left the verandah. As he walked away, his form dissolved into a fine mist and blew away with the wind.

Bloody, bloody man! I fumed. What good was he? He told me nothing!

A few day later, while he worked his way through a four-cup teapot, and more than half of the warm biscuits that I had recently removed from the oven, George proved to be a more attentive listener than Rupert. He raised his eyebrows appreciatively when I related how I had rescued Chance, and ummed and ahhed appropriately when I described my encounter with Dardanelle. He didn't speak, I mean, how could he with his mouth constantly full of tea and biscuits.

As I watched the results of my recent hard work disappear, I groaned inwardly, knowing that, as soon as George left, I would have to make another batch for myself.

Down to his last cup of tea and no biscuits left on the plate (and me not prepared to refill it), George lay back in his chair with a contented sigh, obviously replete.

We were seated in our usual spot on the back verandah. A cool autumnal breeze, with a hint of the promise of winter, eddied around us bringing with it the scent of eucalypts and molasses grass, a weed in Queensland but I loved its fragrance.

Whilst pretending his paws needed a thorough clean, Chance sat on the floor between us and inspected George for several moments. Lowering himself gracefully to the floor, he continued to watch George through heavy eyelids.

'You thought Rupert wasn't much help then,' said George, in the understatement of the year.

'That's putting it mildly,' I huffed. 'Bloody man, he was worse than useless. I thought he would at least tell me how to deal with her.'

'Well, I think he believed you dealt with her as you should. Believe me, Rupert doesn't pull any punches and if he had anything to say or add, he would have. I think your instincts were spot on. Interesting though that he thinks the cat will keep her away.'

'Well,' I laughed. 'She thinks he is my 'familiar',' I told him.

George didn't share in my laughter, and I scowled at him.

'Oh! Come on! You don't believe her!'

'I don't know why you would think that so ludicrous given your current situation,' responded George calmly.

I blinked and glanced at Chance. If cats could grin, that's what the darn cat was doing.

CHAPTER FIFTEEN

As the days passed, the memory of Dardanelle receded to the back of my mind and was swept away entirely by the arrival of Lavender's calf. She came without any fuss or help from me. One morning when I went to do my daily check, I found the calf nestled in the grass, with Lavender standing beside her.

George, on one of his weekly visits, showed me how to handle the new arrival. Lavender didn't seem to mind us being around her baby, as we introduced her to a halter, and I scratched her itchy spots.

Life developed a peaceful rhythm. I collected the eggs the hens generously laid every day and made clumsy attempts to obtain milk from Lavender. She bore my tugging on her teats with stoic indifference. Chance would wait, not so patiently at my side until I put a small amount of milk in a saucer for him, then he would lap, eyes closed until every drop disappeared.

One morning, Chance displayed a restlessness I hadn't seen since he arrived. Several times, he prowled the length of the verandah, a soft growl emanating from his throat before returning to his spot beside the stove. His uneasiness communicated itself to me, concerned Dardanelle lurked somewhere near the house, I carefully surveyed the paddock for any signs of her and found none. The feeling of uneasiness continued, and I retained a sense of alertness as I went about my daily chores.

The day had started off warm, however as the hours passed, the temperature became cooler. The frostiness of winter seemed to want to force itself onto the waning autumnal climate. By mid-afternoon, clad in jeans and jumper, I lit the fire in the combustion stove to warm the house.

An abrupt hiss from Chance heralded the sound of men's voices, arguing loudly.

I followed the commotion to the back verandah where all the noise seemed to be coming from. The sight that greeted me left me speechless, all I could do was stare at the unfolding drama. Beside me, Chance growled and hissed. His tail lashed my legs.

'I'll bloody kill you, you bastard, you shot me!'

The man yelling was thin, almost to the point of emaciation, with long greasy hair, and a greyish blond stubble on his face. His clothes looked like they had not been washed in some time. One hand clutched at his chest; blood oozed through his fingers and blended into his dirt-stained shirt.

'Of course, I bloody shot you, you fool! That's what I came here for. I've had enough of your double dealing. You've taken everything from me! I don't know what you thought you were going to do with that knife you had in your hand, against a gun.'

The other man's voice, though calmer was filled with contempt and a viciousness that chilled me to the bone. He was obviously the better off of the two. Though heavily blood-stained, his clothes were of a better quality, and his pot belly hung over a wide belt.

'The knife that was sticking out of your throat, you mean. The one that you're now holding in *your* hand! So, what do you think of that? Thought you were going to get the better of me, did ya? Thought a gun was better than a knife, didn't ya. Goes to show, ya never watched, 'The Dirty Dozen'. Ha-ha.' The skinny old man cackled.

Astonishment flashed across the face of Potbelly as he stared at the knife in his hand. His other hand flew to his neck, he glanced down at his chest, apparently becoming aware of his blood-soaked clothing for the first time.

In a voice filled with confusion, Potbelly stuttered, 'You ... you ... what have you done?'

'I protected meself, that's what I've done. You got no right comin' round here threatening me with a gun. You jumped up, smart-arse, think you're too bloody good. Think your shit don't stink. Well, I showed ya, didn't I?' Skinny guffawed loudly.

'How? No. You ... you couldn't have. I mean ... I had a gun.'

Potbelly looked at both his hands, then around the ground, searching for a weapon that wasn't there. 'Where's my gun?'

'You dropped it to pull the knife out of your neck. That's when you bled all over that nice shirt of yours,' Skinny chortled. 'Yeh shouldn't have pulled it out, yeh mad bastard. Ha-ha!'

The two men were of a similar age, both around late middle age. Both men were old enough to be my father, *and* old enough to know better.

'That's enough!' I yelled.

They turned to stare at me as if wondering where I had come from, looked back at each other, and then slowly glanced around, as if suddenly aware of their environment.

'Who the bloody hell are you, and how in the flaming hell did we get here?' demanded Potbelly.

'You are on my property now,' I told them firmly. I descended the stairs and made my way over to them.

'Give me that knife.' I glared at them in turn, before holding out my hand to Potbelly.

'Sorry, I ... sorry. How did I get here?' he said, meekly putting the knife, handle-first into my hand.

I decided there was no use pulling any punches with these two idiots. They seemed to have no idea what they had done.

'Well, you have obviously killed each other, haven't you, otherwise you wouldn't be here with me.'

'Killed each other! Dead! We're not bloody dead, we're standing here talking to you,' proclaimed Skinny.

'What are your names?' I asked in an even firmer tone. I couldn't go on thinking of them as Skinny and Potbelly. Not that I told them that, I was pretty sure they wouldn't like it.

'What's yours?' asked Potbelly, with his chin in the air and a gleam of defiance in his eyes.

I had the distinct impression he went through life angry, with a chip on his shoulder.

Taking a deep breath, I said through gritted teeth, 'Mine is Sandrine, but you can call me Sandy. Now tell me your names before I bang your heads together for being such damn fools.'

'Don't you talk to us like that! Who do you think you are? And there'll be no banging our heads together,' said Potbelly.

I could have sworn I had only thought about banging their heads together. God give me strength!

I took another deep breath. 'Where were you two when all this started?'

'Well ... well ...,' Potbelly looked at the ground, up at the sky, anywhere but at me or at Skinny. 'I ...,' he murmured.

'We were at my place,' Skinny interrupted. 'Fred here came storming in with his blasted gun. Thought he was going to teach me a lesson. Didn't ya, just? Hah?'

Well at least I had one name, Fred aka potbelly, shifted from one foot to the other, and scratched his head.

'Well, he owes me money,' he blurted out.

His anger at least appeared to be cooling, I hoped that some semblance of sanity was returning.

'You shot him because he owes you *money*?' I couldn't keep the incredulity from my voice.

'He owes me a *lot* of money. If it wasn't for me ...,'

'Yeah, yeah, if it weren't for you the sky wouldn't be blue ... according to you,' scoffed Skinny, interrupting Fred's tirade.

'We had a deal ...,' began Fred.

'Yeah well, *they* cut you out of the deal, not me,' interrupted Skinny.

'It was my idea!' Objected Fred. 'You wouldn't even had known about it, if it weren't for me.'

'Well, they didn't need access to your property anymore, and maybe if you hadn't lost your flaming temper, they wouldn't have cut you out. So, it serves yourself bloody right. That darn temper of yours has got you into more trouble than you care to admit,' ranted Skinny, jabbing one long, dirty finger in Fred's direction.

'So, you admit you did cut me out!' Huffed Fred, his face suddenly red with veins visibly swelling in his neck.

Skinny was right, anger did seem to be his default emotion.

'*I* didn't cut you out! I just told you why *they* cut you out. It's that bloody anger of yours. Try taking some responsibility for a change. And clean your bloody ears out!' yelled Skinny, looking like he wanted to jump and up down in frustration.

I studied the two men. So bent on continuing their argument, they ignored their wounds, their blood-stained clothing, and their new environment. More importantly, so involved were they in what was obviously a long-standing animosity, it had not occurred to either of them that the wounds they both had suffered, were fatal.

I looked around for any sign that there was help coming.

Apart from a faint mist covering the countryside and the definite drop in temperature, there were no lights that I could attribute to a door opening to the other side. It seemed I was stuck with these angry old men.

CHAPTER SIXTEEN

With one last glance at the two combatants, I turned on my heel and walked away. When they came to their senses they might be interested in listening.

I went into the house while Chance stayed on the verandah, watching the men from the top of the steps. The tip of his tail flicked slowly, and he examined our visitors with narrowed eyes.

The sound of their voices floated through the open window.

'That money is mine by right ....'

'That's all you think about money, money ....'

The scent of jasmine touched my nostrils, and it helped me to detach from the men's argument. Despite knowing the cooler weather would continue until these men passed to the other side, I resisted the urge to close the window to keep the warmth in and block out their voices.

I sighed. Their passing couldn't happen soon enough.

Thankfully, the fire had caught in the combustion stove and a warm kitchen welcomed me. Assembling the makings for coffee, I lit the gas stove; grateful it still worked during times like these.

'I told you not to mess with me ...,' Fred's voice trembled a little.

Was the tone of the argument not as strong? I could only hope as I waited for the kettle to boil.

Taking time to add another block of wood to the stove, and satisfied the fire was going strongly; I returned, coffee in hand to the verandah. Outside, in the cooler air, I wrapped my hands around the hot mug, grateful for its warmth. I sipped the coffee with a part of my mind listening to the men argue, and another part wondering how I was going to cope with them.

Skinny was the first to fall silent and look around properly. Fred was the aggressor, so I guessed that made sense. From what I could piece together, the fight had taken place at Skinny's place, wherever that might be.

'Where the hell am I?' Skinny asked no-one in particular. He took a step backwards, his hand hovering over the wound in his chest.

'I ... what the flamin' hell. I feel strange.' His voice had grown soft, unsure. His knees gave way and Skinny collapsed and lay unmoving, on the ground.

Fred stared at him for a moment, then turned to me with a confused and expectant look on his face. Lifting the cup to my mouth, I returned his gaze. If he thought I was going to rush down there and rescue him, then he could think again.

'I ...I,' Fred stammered. His gaze flicked to Skinny, to me, to his surroundings, then back to Skinny. After another perplexed glance in my direction, his gaze dropped to his shirt front. Tentatively, he touched the blood stains; his hand rose slowly to gingerly explore the wound in his neck before hovering there uncertainly.

Chance turned his head and looked at me inquiringly. I rolled my eyes. Okay, perhaps now was the time for me to get involved. Reluctantly, I put the cup on the table, descended the stairs, and made my way over to the men. Skinny's eyes were open; his vacant expression told me he was not really aware of Fred or me.

'What happened? Where are we?' asked Fred.

'Well, from what I can gather,' I told him with some asperity, 'You two idiots have killed each other. You shot him, and somehow or other, despite being shot he has managed to stab you.'

'Killed? Killed!' Fred's voice became shrill with indignation and disbelief. 'What nonsense!' He blustered. 'I am standing here talking to you, woman. I cannot possibly be dead! Are you insane!'

I was beginning to wonder the same thing myself. Maybe I was insane? Maybe I was hallucinating? Maybe I was having a terrible nightmare and would wake up. Please God, let me wake up. Of course, nothing of the sort happened, and I turned my attention back to what was now my reality.

'Where were you when this happened?' I pointed at their wounds.

'Um, well I went to Jann's house to … well … to …. He owed me money, a lot of money.'

Jann, so that was Skinny's name.

'I didn't mean that.' I said aloud, it was hard to keep an even tone in my voice.

Never had I considered myself a violent person, but at my side, my hand twitched, I wanted to slap him. I curved my fist into a tight ball, took a deep breath and slowly unwound my fingers.

'I mean physically, where were you?'

'Physically?' Fred glanced around. 'Oh right, I see,' he paused, and said with a puzzled look. '*How* did we get here?'

Oh, Dear God!

Groaning inwardly, I took another deep breath and gave myself a mental shake. Best not to hyperventilate.

I tried a different tack, something I hoped would focus his attention. 'Where is Jann's place?'

'Colton,' he named a farming community several hundred kilometres to the west.

Not a local then.

'Where are we?' he asked again.

'Balford,' I told him.

'Balford!' His voice rose several octaves, and he squeaked. 'How the devil did we get here?'

Good question, but how in the hell was I going to answer it.

Since no rational answer came to me, I ignored the question and glanced down at Jann laying on the ground, which begged another question.

How was I going to get him inside?

'Can you carry him inside?' I looked at Fred, whose bluster was evaporating rather quickly now that he appeared to have come to his senses.

Wrong question. I groaned inwardly as Fred's face turned red and his chest began to swell. His anger had returned with a vengeance.

'Humph! Of course, I can but why would I want to? That prick ....'

'Shut Up! I don't want to hear another word about how much money he owes you,' I yelled.

Oh crap, that was no way to handle two newly dead men. Maybe I wasn't cut out for this job? I really needed to find some Zen! Though the shocked look on Fred's face gave me an incredible amount of satisfaction, which I struggled to keep from showing. He looked at me then. I mean really looked. Whatever he saw on my face made him clamp his lips together in one thin white line, and scoop Jann up into his arms.

Jann lay on the bed with his eyes fluttering, awareness appeared to be returning.

Fred stood beside the bed looking decidedly uncomfortable, his eyes darted around the room. 'Where did you say we were?'

I sniffed. How many times must I tell him the same thing? I did my best not to roll my eyes at him, as I covered Jann with the quilt to keep him warm.

'Balford,' I told him again.

'Balford?' He mouthed the name silently, shaking his head with confusion clouding his eyes.

'You can have a bath and clean up. I'll find some clean clothes for you,' I told Fred trying to divert his attention.

'No, I won't,' his bravado had returned. 'I'm going home. My wife will be wondering where I am.'

'Off you go then,' I said, moving past him.

Even if the men didn't eat, I needed to. I began pulling vegetables and some chuck steak from the fridge, thinking I would make a casserole just in case they did eat. Had I been alone my dinner would have consisted of something simpler, but I wanted to keep busy and think. John had been different; I thought I was looking after an injured man not a dead one. Thankfully his exit to the other side had happened quickly. What I was going to do with these two, I had no idea.

Various chores, that needed attending, passed through my mind. The fridge wouldn't stay cold for too long. Lucky there wasn't a lot of meat in the freezer. I would have to put water in the cooler on the verandah, so that I could transfer some of the contents from the fridge to it, and the cooler weather would help as well.

'How *do* I get back home?' demanded Fred, coming out of the spare bedroom and interrupting my mental sorting of everything that would need doing.

Hands on his hips with feet spaced widely apart, he looked like he was ready for another fight, only with me this time. It was going to take all the patience I could muster to deal with this man.

I took another deep breath. Deep breathing was all I seemed to be doing since these two arrived. Resisting the urge to wave it in his face, I put down the knife. After all he had already killed one man. Could he kill me? Can the dead kill the living? My grandmother's letter had said I wasn't in any danger. Had she ever had to deal with fools like these two? Of course she had, and I was sure she had coped better than I was at the moment.

'I've got no idea,' I told him. 'I suggest you have a bath and get some of that blood off you. It stinks.'

I had never before noticed that blood stank so much.

'The shower won't work now, there won't be enough pressure. I'll find some clothes for you,' I said, returning to the spare bedroom to rummage through the cupboard.

It was Fred's turn to sniff, but whatever was on his mind, vanished before it reached his lips; instead, he nodded his acquiescence and followed me silently to the bathroom.

Fred came out of the bathroom looking and smelling like a different man. The clothes I had provided were not as good a quality as his own, however he wore them with the air of a man who radiated self-importance. His thick thatch of greying, mousy brown hair was neatly combed, and he appeared to have recovered an evenness of mind. He was calmer, more composed.

In the oven, the casserole gently bubbled. I offered Fred a glass of wine, which he declined.

'I wouldn't mind a cup of tea, though,' he suggested politely.

A new man, it seemed. Maybe one I could like, though it would have been idiotic of me to think that the angry man I had seen earlier had disappeared. After all, his anger had caused him to shoot a man, over money. For now, I was prepared to give him the benefit of the doubt.

'I wouldn't mind one either,' said Jann from the doorway. He didn't look too steady on his legs, so I pulled a chair close to him, and he sank into it with a grateful look on his face.

'I wouldn't mind a bath also.' Jann's glance, from beneath rather long blond eyelashes, was hopeful. He seemed almost shy.

Fred grunted, a quick look at his face told me Jann's presence had ignited his temper again. He stomped past me out to the back deck. His heavy footsteps clomped around the verandah several times, then I heard him thump down the stairs.

With his absence, a smidgeon of peace eased its way into my body. I took a deep breath that was different from the many other deep breaths that I had dragged into my lungs in an effort to calm myself. Releasing the breath slowly, I found the equilibrium that had disappeared with the men's arrival.

Bloody Fred was stress on two legs. While I had no doubt his wife was wondering where he'd got to, I was equally sure she was enjoying the peace of his absence.

Not my problem. My problem was dealing with them until they left. What was taking so long? Where were these spirits from the other side? Maybe part of the trouble was neither Jann nor Fred realised they *were* dead? John seemed to have realised something was wrong, he kept wanting to go back. Back to where though? To his body? Maybe? How could I get Fred and Jann to grasp that?

Chance's ferociously long yowl sent my already strained nervous system into overdrive, it felt like every hair on my body was standing to attention. Loud running footsteps, preceded Fred bursting headlong into the kitchen; struggling for breath, terror filled his eyes.

'There's a ... a woman. I think it's a woman. She ... she's dead,' he panted.

His eyes rolled upwards into his head, and he fainted sprawling out on the kitchen floor.

I stepped over him and went outside. Dardanelle was standing (or floating, I couldn't decide which) in the orchard. A smile that sent shivers up my spine played around her lips. Her luminous eyes held mine for several seconds, before she slowly faded and disappeared.

Leaving Chance crouched and on guard at the top of the steps, I went back into the kitchen. Stepping over Fred's inert body I went to find a lamp to illuminate the dark verandah.

Hanging the lamp under the eaves on the verandah, I called, 'Rupert, I could do with some help, or at least some advice.'

The deep chested, disjointed hissing sound of a possum interrupted the silence of the night and helped to remind me that I was dealing with the twin aspects of existence – life and death.

When Rupert didn't appear, I returned to Fred, who was still out cold on the kitchen floor. Since I couldn't move him, I threw a blanket over him and went to draw a bath for Jann. He was still sitting at the table, his hands wrapped around the teacup, staring vacantly into space.

After running his bath, I didn't rouse Jann from his reverie to hasten his bathing, he obviously wasn't ready. We sat together in silence, watching Fred sprawled out on the floor. There seemed to be nothing either of us wanted to say. The old clock ticked loudly in the ensuing silence, which for me marked the minutes until Rupert arrived.

What *was* taking him so long?

Why had Dardanelle chosen now to return?

What had she said or done to make Fred so scared?

Where the bloody hell was Rupert?

'Can I have that bath now?' Jann asked somewhat timidly.

My gaze switched to him, and he seemed to shrink from it. I must have been glaring. Mentally, I gave myself another shake, it seemed I had been doing that a lot today.

'Sorry, of course,' I told him.

With Jann in the bath, I turned my attention to Fred. There was no way Jann, nor I, would be able to get him into a bed. He was too heavy. He would have to stay on the floor until he recovered. I looked around hopefully for any signs of help from the other side.

Crickets.

I slumped back into my chair and poured another cup of tea

CHAPTER SEVENTEEN

The house was quiet when I woke the following morning. I lay snuggled deep beneath the covers of my warm comfortable bed, straining to hear any sound from my visitors.

Chance had burrowed under the blankets and was curled up beside my leg. If he wasn't worried, then neither was I. It was too much to hope that those two had crossed over during the night. The house was cold and that was enough to let me know that at least one of the men was still in the house - unfortunately.

It had been close to midnight before I was able to settle the men and climb into bed myself.

After his bath, Jann sipped at a second cup of tea, (his first cup lay untouched) though he refused to eat. Shampoo had revealed his shoulder length hair to be blond, with hints of grey throughout. Long blond lashes framed clear blue eyes, and I saw the remnants of what once had been a very good-looking man. There was a gentleness about him that the anger, dirt, and blood had obscured. The tranquillity of his personality was in sharp contrast to Fred's bulldozing persona.

He said very little, just watched me with a confused look in his eyes. Several times it seemed he was on the verge of speaking but each time he stopped himself, shook his head and gazed around confusedly. After a long time of staring at me, he nodded as if he had come to a decision.

'Do you mind if I go to bed now, missus?'

Unsteady on his feet, Jann needed my help to stand. I guided him to the bedroom and helped him into bed. He fell asleep instantly.

I hovered for a moment, watching and waiting for any signs of his impending departure.

No such luck.

With a stomach growling from lack of food, I returned to the kitchen.

I was eating a very late dinner when Fred finally opened his eyes and looked apprehensively about the room. When he caught sight of me, his eyes widened in recognition and alarm.

Fred's hands rose slowly to his neck. He touched his wound lightly before carefully feeling all around his body. Abruptly, his hands flopped to his sides, and he lay as if shocked for several moments, staring at the ceiling.

Surreptitiously, I watched him and continued eating. He scowled at me, rolled over and on wobbly legs, regained his feet and made his way over to the table to sit facing me.

'Thanks for the help,' he growled.

'You're welcome,' I replied calmly.

He studied me with bleary eyes for a long moment before dropping his head into his hands.

'Where did you say we were?' he said to the table.

'Balford.'

'Are you hungry?' I asked.

He lifted his head and considered for a moment. 'No. Yes ... maybe. What is there to eat?'

'Casserole. What I'm eating now.'

'Humph. Smells alright. Okay, I'll have some.'

I stared at him in silence for several seconds; this man was a bully, and he was not going to bully me.

He grimaced. 'Please?'

We ate without speaking once I had put a plateful of casserole in front of him, it seemed he was hungry after all.

Fred pushed his plate away after he had wiped it clean with a slice of bread. 'Where is he?'

'If you mean Jann, he is sleeping.'

Fred considered this for a moment. He glanced around the room, then back at me with an appraising look.

'Who was that woman?'

'Her name is Dardanelle. Best to stay clear of her. What did she say to frighten you.'

He looked at me askance, 'She's a *ghost*. Why would you think she could *talk*? She's dead! Isn't that scary enough?'

He hadn't listened to a word I said about him and Jann being dead. I released a deep sigh and held my peace. He would learn soon enough, and I would have no need for words.

'Uhm,' he murmured, looking suddenly tired. 'Where am I sleeping?'

'On the couch, there is only one spare bed.'

'I am not sleeping on the couch,' he proclaimed loudly. 'Turf him out of that bed,' he said with a jerk of his head, indicating the spare room. 'He can sleep on the bloody couch.'

I blew air through my nose in frustration and glared at the vexatious man sitting at my table. With an angry push, I shoved the chair backwards and away from the table, before leaving to gather up the necessary bed linen.

Placing clean sheets on the lounge, along with a couple of warm blankets and a pillow, I turned to Fred who had been following me, 'Jann is asleep and even if he wasn't, I'm not changing the sheets on the bed, so you would have to sleep in his dirty sheets. Would you like that?'

The look he gave me told me he was wondering how far he could push me. The glare I returned told him not very far. He lowered himself onto the lounge, swept the blankets over himself and closed his eyes.

Bloody Rupert never showed, so I went to bed.

I had finished breakfast and was enjoying a second cup of coffee, when Jann stepped out onto the verandah, yawning widely, and rubbing his face. He stumbled over to the table and lowered himself into the chair opposite me.

'So, it wasn't a dream then.'

I shrugged and nodded. We sat in silence and Jann gazed around the countryside.

'Where did you say we were?'

'Balford.'

'Okay,' he nodded absently, 'Crikey. This is a bit flamin' strange.'

Don't I know it.

'Would you like some coffee or tea?'

'Tea please, I don't drink coffee. If you wouldn't mind, that is? Finish your own first.'

Right then and there, I decided I liked the man.

Fred appeared in the kitchen as I was preparing tea for Jann.

'Would you like a cup?' I asked, indicating the tray I had prepared.

'I'll have a coffee ... please.'

Liking Fred was a lot harder. Why did the please have to be an afterthought? Didn't this man have *any* manners? I fumed silently.

Where was bloody Rupert? Shouldn't he be here by now?

How was I going to deal with these men? They seemed to have no notion that they were dead. The questions tumbled around inside my head and the answers were elusive as ever.

Fred followed me out to the back deck to join Jann. I placed the tray on the table and left the men sitting on the verandah, while I went to check on Lavender and her calf.

In the kerfuffle surrounding the arrival of Fred and Jann, I hadn't locked the calf away for the night, so there was no milking this morning. Chance was beside me as usual as I made my rounds of the animals; he usually shadowed me, though I figured he too must want to get away from the men.

The morning was crisp, the sun had just topped the highest trees, and its weak rays spread a soft glow over the countryside.

I made my way down to the front gate. Chance often ran at my heels or at other times went exploring. There was no sign of Rupert at the gate as I had been hoping. We retraced our steps and joined Fred and Jann on the verandah. Chance gave each of the men an imperious glance before sauntering inside.

The walk had cleared my mind and helped dissipate most of the pent-up tension I held within my body. I needed to listen to the part of me that knew there was a process to this strange situation and as much as I wanted to, I couldn't force their departure. My job was to relax and help them, not wish them gone before they were ready to go.

Jann surprisingly took the lead, 'I think we might be ready to listen now.'

Fred gave a sceptical humph but otherwise appeared to agree with Jann. Or at least, he didn't start one of his tantrums which he obviously used to get his own way.

'How do you both feel?' I asked, not wanting to attempt to explain something that I barely understood myself.

'I don't feel any different,' announced Fred.

Jann rolled his eyes and gave him a disbelieving look. Fred's face went red, but before he could launch into one of his rants, I snapped, 'That's enough. Your anger will achieve nothing here.'

'But I don't feel any different!' he insisted, waving his arms around.

'You're not worried? Even a little,' I queried.

'I'm a little worried but I don't *feel* any different,' explained Fred.

So, worry wasn't a feeling for Fred, I mulled over that for a bit then asked, 'What has changed for you then?'

'Well ... Well obviously, there's *something* wrong,' he postured. 'I have no idea how to go home, and when I think about it, there appears to be some sort of disconnect that I can't explain.'

'That's what I feel,' interjected Jann. 'A disconnect. Like ... I can't go back. But I don't know where to go from here. It's feels like I'm waiting.'

A chill spread over my body at Jann's words, they were so similar to John's, they left me speechless. Chance appeared beside me, and sat staring at Jann, a soft rumbling in his chest.

'Oh!' Jann said softly. 'I think they're coming. I can ... feel ....' His voice softened and faded.

'What are,' began Fred.

I raised my hand to Fred, stopping him from continuing.

'Do you need to lie down?' I asked Jann.

'No. No ... it won't be long now,' whispered Jann, even as he spoke, a soft glow emerged from his solar plexus.

A sudden movement from Fred had me reaching across the table to grasp his hand. He calmed at my touch. I flicked a glance at him and saw horror dawning in his eyes and across his face. A quick shake of my head warned him to stillness.

The light that enveloped the house should have been blinding, instead it brought with it such an intense feeling of tranquillity and wonderment that it was impossible to look away. The trickle of light, leaking from Jann's body, floated towards the radiance. When the lights linked, the trickle became a torrent; then with a silent explosion, Jann and the light were gone, and Fred was screaming in horror.

CHAPTER EIGHTEEN

'But *where* did he go?' Fred asked for what seemed like the mil-
lionth time.

I paused in my third attempt to light the copper, and looked long-
ingly at the washing machine, which didn't work now that I had a visitor.

Washing clothes had become an odious chore. I sent a silent ac-
knowledgment of deep respect to the generation of women who had
used this antiquated, difficult method of cleaning the household linen.

'Fred! I've already told you!'

I had lost patience with him days ago, regained it and lost it again,
several times. Nothing was working, now resignation resided inside of
me, and once again I was doing by best to explain something, about
which I knew very little.

'He passed to the other side. That's as much as I know. As I have
already told you many times, this house is like a portal that gives souls
that have been yanked from their body, time to adjust before transcend-
ing. People with long illnesses, have time to adjust. People like you and
Jann, (who stupidly kill each other, I thought, but didn't say) don't have
time.'

'I don't want that to happen to me,' his voice was filled with anxiety
and fear.

'There's no rush, Fred. It'll happen when you're ready, not before.' I
said in an effort to reassure him - *again*.

Though as far as I was concerned, it couldn't happen fast enough.
He was not good company. He was self-absorbed, often rude and anger
lived, like an extra layer, beneath the surface of his skin.

'I want to go back to my wife.'

'You've tried that, how many times now?'

'But I was a terrible husband. I know that now. I want to go back and ... and ... start again. Say I'm sorry. I ... Oh dear God, I've been such a fool!'

Ring lifeline, tell somebody who cares, I wanted to say but didn't. It seemed like there was a lot I wanted to say and didn't. Bloody Rupert still hadn't put in an appearance, and I had given up expecting him.

The fire had gone out again. I lit another match and touched it to the paper that hadn't burnt.

'Maybe that's what's holding you back?' I suggested. 'Wanting to make amends when it's too late. Was Jann married?'

He sniffed and turned his head away. I'd asked him this question once before, trying to understand why Jann had been able to transcend so quickly. Fred's volatile reaction had been out of all proportion to the relatively simple question.

'Where do you think souls go when they die?' I asked in sudden in-spiration. I had never explored this question with him before. Fred had bombarded me with questions, maybe it was time to explore his own beliefs.

'Well. Well, I didn't think there *was* anything after this life,' he said slowly, uncertainly.

This life? He was no longer part of *this* life. I glanced up at him.

'Fred, what do you think is happening here?' I asked, watching the last of the paper burn to ashes.

Using a small rake, I dragged out all the half-burnt kindling I had put under the copper, and using fresh twigs, started building it again.

'I don't know! I don't bloody know!' he wailed.

Tearing an old newspaper into strips, I poked a couple of pieces between the kindling and applied a lit match to the paper. The paper caught alight, I added a bit more paper and some small pieces of wood.

Fred whimpered something inaudibly. Chance suddenly appeared at my side; he had been absent most of the morning. I gave him a side-ways glance and continued to feed larger pieces of wood to the fire and sighed with relief as it at last, caught and held. Chance growled and I stood, putting my hands against my back to stretch the kinks out of it from bending over for so long.

Goosebumps wrapped my body in a sudden chill. Dardanelle stood only a few metres away.

'You're not welcome here, Dardanelle,' I told her.

'I not come for you,' she said scornfully. Her eyes were fixed on Fred.

'But this man, he may join me.' An enticing smile played around her lips.

'Leave,' I ordered her.

A throaty laughter greeted my words as she moved a little closer.

Chance stalked forward and stood between the wraith and Fred and I. She hesitated and scowled at him.

'My offer holds true,' she told Fred before turning and drifting away.

'She *can* talk! Why can I see her? Who *is* she?'

'She's a soul who refuses to cross. I very much doubt her intentions are good,' I told him.

'I've never been able to see ghosts before. Why can I see them now? She scares the bejesus of me,' he shivered as he spoke.

I didn't answer his questions. I figured he knew; he just didn't want to admit that he knew.

'Yeah well, she doesn't exactly fill me with light and laughter,' I told him.

Dardanelle's appearance seemed to leave both Fred and I in a state of alertness. He spent the rest of the day following me around and looking over his shoulder. I watched Chance, knowing that he was the best indicator of her presence.

Late one afternoon, a few days after our encounter with Dardanelle, we were sitting on the verandah. I was enjoying an after-dinner wine. Fred had stopped eating a couple of days ago. A glass of wine lay on the table in front of him. He'd picked it up, sniffed, and put the glass down again many times without tasting.

'He married the girl I loved. He stole her from me.' Fred said suddenly.

I nodded encouragingly and said nothing. His mood had changed. There was a mellowness to it that I hadn't seen before.

'We were teenage sweethearts. I thought we would marry. Jann was my best friend,' His voice trailed off as if he'd lost his train of thought in a sudden memory.

At last, I understood the animosity he held for Jann. It had very little to do with the money he thought he was owed, and more to do with the love he'd lost.

Fred sat in silence with a careworn, beleaguered expression in his eyes.

'Were they happy together?' I asked, hoping to bring Fred back to the present, and get him to release some of the demons that held him stuck to a life he was no longer a part of.

A thunderous look passed across Fred's face, before he uttered through clamped teeth, 'Yes, very.'

'Why does that upset you?'

'I'm not upset,' he asserted.

The tension showing in his face and body told a different story. I ignored him and took another sip of wine. A gentle breeze eddied around the verandah, bringing with it the scent of grass and wood smoke.

'I *can't* stay here,' Fred said suddenly, his voice filled with anguish. 'And I can't go where he went. I just can't. You see that don't you.'

He looked around, searching wildly, 'I must go back to my wife. I love her. I do. I always have, but I just. Oh God what have I done?' Fred groaned, resting his head on his arms.

Much to my horror, he started sobbing.

Crying men were out of my comfort zone. With no idea of what to say or do, I sipped wine while he blubbered. Chance rose and stretched, then moved silently indoors; evidently a crying man was not something he wanted to deal with either. I watched him go with something akin to envy.

The night crept in softly around us, with only the lantern light from the kitchen window, fragmenting the dark. I could barely see Fred's face, and it might have been this, that finally encouraged him to tell his story.

'Annie and Jann *were* happy,' Fred said, with more than a hint of disappointment in his voice. 'I could have been too, but I was so busy wanting what I thought was mine and what I had lost, that I ... I treated Grace as second best. She wasn't. She wasn't,' he groaned.

I tensed and hoped he wasn't going to cry again. He'd only just recovered from his latest crying bout.

It was a relief when he exclaimed, 'What a fool! What a bloody fool I've been!'

His anger had returned, and I realised I was more at ease with his anger than his grief. What that said about me, I didn't examine too closely; it could wait for another day.

Fred stopped speaking and seemed to lose himself in thought. I took the opportunity to retrieve the bottle of wine from the cooler on the verandah and pour myself another glass. I definitely needed two glasses for this.

'I don't know why Grace hasn't left me. I've been angry with Annie and Jann for so long, that I've neglected her. I haven't realised what I've had, until now.' Fred said in a soft, anguished voice.

I noticed he was still talking in the present tense, but I didn't correct him.

'Jann got everything,' Fred couldn't keep the bitterness from his voice. 'Annie, his farm thrived. While I got Grace ... and my farm. Our farm ... we struggled, we've always struggled.'

Which I thought was an odd thing to say, seeing as how he appeared to be the more prosperous of the two.

'Annie died five years ago, and Jann hasn't been the same since. He's let himself and the farm go. But even though he didn't care, the money still came to him. To *him*, when it was my idea,' resentment had returned to his voice.

I tried not to roll my eyes and failed, obviously a bad habit that I would have to deal with - or not.

Driven by emotions that constantly fluctuated, Fred was back thinking about the money he thought he had lost - *again*. But now I knew why Jann was able to cross quicker than Fred.

It was late by the time we went to bed.

Fred moved into the spare room after Jann left and I spared him a thoughtful, sympathising glance as he shut the door behind him. He'd allowed his life and the life of his family to be coloured by anger and disappointment.

Now it was too late to make amends.

CHAPTER NINETEEN

I woke abruptly and alert. My heartbeat had ratcheted up a notch but was not beating wildly.

Unsure as to what had woken me, I lay still in the dark room and listened intently. What had dragged me, so rudely, from my sleep? The now familiar, night-time sounds of the bush greeted me.

Distantly, a possum screeched and hissed. Closer an owl hooted, while nearby the mournful cry of a curlew drifted through the open window.

My eyes adjusted slowly to the shadows in the room. Living in the bush, with the only light being from the moon, was different from living in a city filled with light. The soft glow of a half-moon reduced the inky blackness of the night and allowed me to dimly see the furniture in the room.

Chance's hissing spit was full of menace, and I realised he was not on the bed with me. I threw back the covers and slid from the bed. Reaching for the torch, I didn't turn it on. I had learned that oftentimes the eyes adjusted quickly, and it was easier to see in the dark without a light, especially if I too didn't want to be discovered.

The door to the spare room stood wide open, a quick glance revealed that Fred was not in the bed.

Soft footed, I moved to the verandah. The first thing I saw was Dardanelle, drifting in the shadows close to the house. Chance, hackles raised and with claws unsheathed, stood at the top of stairs. He was not facing the wraith, instead he was preventing Fred from descending the stairs.

'Leave Dardanelle,' I ordered. 'You are not welcome here.'

The wraith drifted backwards a short distance. Her eyes held an expectant predatory look, and her gaze was fixed on Fred.

'No! I want to go with her. I can't leave Grace. I can't!' Fred wailed.

'That woman cannot take you to Grace,' I told him sternly, striking a match and lighting the kerosene lamp I kept on the table. Its narrow glow splintered the darkness.

'She said she can. She spoke to me. She said she can,' pleaded Fred, looking around wildly.

'She lied Fred! She can't take you to your wife. Grace would not be able to see you, and if she could, she would see your ghostly self, and that would probably just frighten her.'

'Frighten her? No! No, I wouldn't frighten her. I wouldn't,' he whimpered.

'You would, Fred,' I insisted in a firm voice. Then with as soft a tone as I could manage, I repeated. 'You would. Grace will *not* be able to see you, and if she can sense a presence, she may not know that it is you. Think about this, please.'

A stillness settled over Fred, he stood up straighter, my pleas seemed to have reached him. Chance however, increased his growling and made ready to spring. Which gave me pause. What could Chance perceive that I could not?

'Chance,' I whispered, 'chase the woman, not Fred.' His ears flicked at my words.

They moved together but Chance was quicker, he leapt to the verandah railing and down to the ground with all the grace and swiftness of his kind. Fred's leap was awkward, he lurched over the side, falling to the ground in an untidy heap, before struggling clumsily to regain his feet.

The hissing, spitting feline didn't break his stride, when his paws touched the ground, Chance ferociously launched himself at Dardanelle, who fled.

Without hesitation, Chance spun in Fred's direction then moved into a hunting crouch, stalking slowly towards Fred, whose face became suddenly etched with terror.

Like the wraith, Fred bolted, regaining the steps and the verandah in a flurry of panicked movements. He fell into one of the chairs, pleading between gasping breaths, 'Keep him away from me. Keep him away.'

Chance moved stealthily up the stairs and regarded the trembling man through slitted eyelids. Several of my heartbeats later he sat, and licked his paws in what I thought was a very self-satisfied manner.

Struggling to keep the grin from my face, I considered Fred in silence for a moment, before turning my attention to the opaque night.

Overhead, stars lit the sky like tiny fireflies.

I waited, listening to Fred's effort to steady his breathing, and watched for Dardanelle's return. In the waiting, my mind quietened, and my thoughts turned to questioning why I was trying to save this man from his own judgements. It seemed right to urge him to cross over when really it wasn't my decision - it was his. While Dardanelle's presence frightened me, and I questioned her motives for trying to entice Fred away, it wasn't my choice to make.

Where was bloody Rupert when I needed him?

That was a constant thought of mine lately.

When morning came, Fred was sitting on the verandah in the same place I had left him the night before. He appeared morose with an air of such sadness that I, very briefly, felt sorry for him. Fred's inability to accept things as they were, seemed to colour his whole life. He hadn't accepted that Annie loved Jann, and in the process, he had lost their friendship. Fred had also chosen to see the woman he married and who loved him, as second best. Worst of all, he's refusal to accept that he had not profited from a business deal, had led him to murder.

What a mess.

Making myself a coffee, I sat opposite Fred. He didn't acknowledge me, he barely even moved. I sipped my coffee and allowed the serenity of the cool morning to wash over me like a gentle wave.

During the long, sleep evading night, I had worried over the events of the evening.

Why was I trying to protect the man?

And who from?

Himself?

Dardanelle?

I reread my grandmother's letter, hoping to find an answer and came at last to a solution, and hoped for all concerned, it was the right one.

Now, I had to share my decision with Fred.

'The choice to leave or stay is yours, I will no longer interfere,' I told him. 'But know this, if you leave this house and go to the wraith, you cannot return without my permission.'

Fred's unfocused gaze remained on the table for several minutes, he didn't lift his head or react to my comment, I wasn't even sure he had heard. I placed my empty coffee cup on the table and made ready to leave. I had a cow to milk and chickens to feed and release from their pen.

Fred lifted his head, 'I can go?'

'Yes. Of course, you always could. I just didn't want you to go with the ghost.' I didn't want to say her name, it made her sound as if she walked in the flesh and was real.

'Yes, but,' Fred began.

'I'm not discussing this with you, Fred. You know your choices. We've been over them many times. Now, it's your decision.'

Frustrated with him, I left him sitting there and went about my daily chores.

Two nights later, I was woken by something, none too gently, swatting my face. I didn't need to open my eyes to know that it was Chance's paw batting my nose. He growled softly, suddenly I was wide awake and rising from my bed. Chance and I crept past the empty spare bedroom and out to the kitchen.

The door leading to the verandah was open. We stood in the doorway, watching Fred slowly descend the stairs. Dardanelle waited for him with a triumphant gleam in her eyes and a spine-chilling smirk on her lips.

With an enormous effort, I stayed silent. I had told him it was his choice to make, and apparently and appallingly, he had chosen the wraith.

Fred stood on the ground at the bottom of the stairs, hesitated and glanced back. For several long minutes his gaze rested on me. At first, I saw determination in his eyes, then confusion and indecision before he turned away. One hand clung to the handrail, he swayed backward and forward, then unexpectedly, sat on the bottom step.

An annoyed and uncertain expression developed on Dardanelle's face, her eyes flicked to me, hatred flashed in them, and a moment later she disappeared.

A miniscule ray of light exuded from Fred's body, and I breathed a sigh of relief. They came for him then, only this time I saw radiant figures in the light.

CHAPTER TWENTY

Two days later, I took my morning coffee out to the verandah and found Rupert puffing contentedly on his pipe.

Annoyance flashed through me at the sight of him.

'You're a bit bloody late,' I told him.

A smile touched his lips and was gone, though a twinkle remained in his brown eyes. He removed the pipe and said, 'Thinking you needed me, didn't make it so.'

'Humph! I could have used your support,' I grouched, savouring the first sip of my coffee and feeling slightly more alert because of it.

'I think not or else I would have been here. You have done well.'

'What would have happened if he had gone with that woman?'

Rupert gave a small shrug of his shoulders, 'Some eventually cross. Others wander with purpose. Others ...,' his voice became sad, wistful, 'become part of the lost.'

He puffed and I waited until he continued. 'There is always hope, but that is for others to concern themselves with. Do not trouble yourself with something that is outside of your power to control. The decision to leave or stay, as you quite rightly determined, is theirs, not yours.'

'How did you know I had decided that?'

He raised a quizzical eyebrow at me, and I fell silent. Bloody, bloody man.

Chance joined us and stretched out on the floor between Rupert and me. He looked like a cat, contented with his lot.

'He is indeed your familiar,' observed Rupert.

'For him to be my familiar, wouldn't that make me a witch?'

'An old term, merely meaning wise woman. Their magic lay in their knowledge, though some perhaps found access to the power of the ancients. Have you not just proved yourself wise?'

I rolled my eyes and grunted at him in disbelief. I very much doubted that I had proved myself anything close to wise. The experience with Jann and Fred had left me shaken. My feelings ranged from drained, astonished, and second guessing myself.

Not for the first time, I wished Mum had had the courage to be honest with me - before she became ill. I also wished I had taken more notice of her when she did try to tell me. She had never been one to make up stories; in fact, when I thought about it, she was often brutally honest. Yes, she had her secrets, but now that I understood some of those secrets, I didn't blame her. It wasn't as if I was prepared to tell anyone of my current situation. What if they decided I needed a mental health review, which, come to think of it, wouldn't be a bad idea.

'You will recover,' said Rupert. 'These feelings will pass, and in time, the impact of these visits will lessen. For one without the guidance of the generations, you have proved yourself more than worthy and capable. Know that we are proud.'

My mouth fell open in surprise, I shut it with a sudden snap that jarred my jaws.

'How could you ...,' I began.

Rupert stood and made his way towards the stairs. Before he reached the bottom of the steps, he disappeared.

Blast the man!

As usual, George proved to be a more sympathetic listener.

I was ushering Beetle, (as I had named Lavender's calf), into her pen late the following afternoon, when I spied him and his dogs, moving throughout the orchard. George was picking the last of the crop of fruit and placing them in a bag that he carried.

At the sight of George's dogs, Jack and Sally, Chance jumped up onto the bail's railings. A low, warning growl coming from deep within his chest, told me he was not scared. I only hoped the dogs had the sense not to engage.

'If you don't want these, I'll take them home and make some jam,' George said, as he reached the bails.

The dogs, who had followed along behind George, took one, long, calculating look at Chance, and retreated to the safety of the orchard.

A wise choice.

George watched them go with a grin, then turned back to me.

'So long as I get some of the jam,' I told him with a smile.

His dark eyes smiled back. The wind played with his hair, lifting black strands and letting them fall where they may, leaving an untidy mess in its wake. His neatly trimmed beard eluded the wind's touch, and I resisted the urge to reach out and run my fingers through his unruly hair.

'Of course, that's a fair trade,' he told me. 'You supply the fruit, and I do all the work.'

'Stop whining,' I replied.

George grinned and my heart wobbled.

Ensuring she had water for the night, I shut the gate behind Beetle.

'Took a while for your last visitors to go,' remarked George as we made our way towards the house.

I glanced up at him and nodded.

Chance walked beside us, while Jack and Sally, followed along behind and were smart enough to keep a safe distance away.

'How are you feeling?' asked George.

'Drained,' I replied, casting him a curious glance, 'How did you know how long they were here for?'

'The place is shielded when you have visitors. I can't see the house or the property for that matter. No one can. In days gone by, according to Rupert, if anyone came who meant harm to the guardian, they simply could not find the property. So, you see I always know when you have a visitor.'

'People in the district seem to know about the place, though,' I said, remembering John's funeral and his parents.

'For most of the people in the district, it's an old wife's tale. Some believe, some don't. It's the way of most things. I understand in the beginning, everyone believed, and the guardian held a respected and sometimes feared place in the community.'

'You seem to know a lot about it.'

'I was friends with Vivienne. We had a lot of long chats; it's a shame you didn't know her.'

'Speaking of Vivienne, who looked after her mail and bills. Obviously, there were times when she couldn't.'

'Harriet Gould was not only her friend, but she also dealt with all her personal business as well.'

'Thanks, I might see if she will do the same for me.'

Silence fell between us as I contemplated his relationship with Vivienne. I would have loved to have known her, and to be able to talk to her. There was so much I could have learnt. I longed to know more about my family of women who so fearlessly (or not) guided the dead to the afterlife. I didn't blame Mum, but a small part of me wished she hadn't let fear dictate her life, and in turn, mine.

'Are you sure you're alright?' George asked suddenly, stopping, and turning towards me. 'How about seeing a movie and having dinner with me tomorrow night.'

I regarded him in silence for a moment, and then said hesitatingly, 'I would love to go to a movie and have dinner with you, George, but not if it's a date or something even resembling a 'date'. I....'

'Whoa, hold up there cowgirl,' exclaimed George, backing away with his hands in the air. 'Friends. Just friends. I didn't want to tell you this, but you look as if you need a hug, and a week of sleep. In short, you look bloody awful.'

Dumbfounded by his outburst, and how accurately he had intuited my feelings, I burst into tears.

George dropped the bag of fruit on the ground, and enveloped me in one of his wonderfully, generous hugs. Clinging to George, I wept away the anxiety, uncertainty, and fears that I had held inside since Fred's departure. Feeling safe in his arms, I clung to him long after the last sob had left my body.

Eventually, I took one last shuddering breath, and reluctantly, released myself from his embrace.

I stepped away, glanced up and our eyes held, 'George,' I whispered. 'Oh George, thank you,' and stepped back into his arms.

His arms enveloped me, holding me gently, I felt his lips brush the top of my head. Despite my protestations, I wished that tomorrow was a date.

CHAPTER TWENTY-ONE

Harriet regarded me for too long an interval with her sharp, intelligent eyes. It occurred to me she used silence as a weapon. Since I was good at silence myself, it didn't bother me.

'You look better than the last time I saw you.' Was her assessment when she finally spoke.

'I do feel better, but I didn't come to discuss how I feel with you,' I told her, wondering why I suddenly felt like we'd become combatants.

A light, that could have been a smile, flashed across her eyes and was gone. It didn't touch her lips, so the impression was fleeting.

When next she spoke, her tone had a definite softness to it. 'You *do* remind me of Vivienne. You have her spirit. I've decided I like you, so how can I help.'

'Do you only help people you like?'

Ignoring my question, Harriet reached for her phone and asked, 'Would you like a coffee? I'm about to place an order.'

'Ah, um ... yes please.' The abrupt switch in her manner, caught me off guard.

'And to answer your question. Yes. I have learnt not to surround myself with people I find difficult to be around. They not only irritate and confuse, but they can also have a negative impact on one's health. Trust me, I speak from experience.'

Since I wasn't sure that needed a reply, I launched into why I had come to see her. 'I understand you took care of Vivienne's bills and personal affairs. Since there are times when I won't be able to, I was hoping you might do the same for me.'

I paused then added, 'Also, I want to change my last name to Legg.'

If she was surprised by my request to change my name, it didn't show by even a micro expression on her face.

'I am more than happy to take care of your affairs,' she replied. 'Vivienne had a special account set up for me with her bank, and we can do the same, so that is no problem. Now, tell me why you want to change your name.'

To control my irritation with her nosiness, I hesitated before replying, 'I've thought about this a lot, and it's something Beatrice Milledge said to me about the legacy of the Legg women.'

Harriet raised an eyebrow and remained silent.

'Come!' She called in answer to a tap on the door. Our coffees had arrived.

The coffee was delicious. The tension between us eased and eventually I restarted the conversation, 'I guess I want the association with the Legg women to continue. I have no great affiliation with my father's name of Parker. He barely deserves to be called a 'father', since the name itself implies so much more.'

Harriet placed her cup on the table, and gave me another one of her long, silent assessing looks.

I returned the favour until I grew irritable, and changed the subject, 'Do you know where my grandmother is buried?'

The question disrupted her silence. She picked up her cup, took a few sips, then replied, 'She wasn't buried. Vivienne was cremated, like all the Legg women. None of them were buried. Their ashes are spread across the land you now own.'

'*All* of them? How? When did the first crematorium come here?'

'In the beginning, which was around the late eighteen hundreds, there wasn't a crematorium. The story goes that Violet's daughter, Verna, built a funeral pyre and cremated her mother on the land.'

'How much do you know about my family history?'

Harriet placed her cup on the table and turned to her computer. Coffee break was over.

As she worked, Harriet told me, 'Most of it is oral history. Very little of it can be verified by public documentation. However, the community was so fascinated by the women, the stories have been passed down. Unfortunately, none of your family kept a written history.

Though I very much doubt it would have been believed and could very well have had them committed to a mental health facility.'

That certainly had a ring of truth. If I ever wrote about my experiences, it would be as a novel. I shifted restlessly in my chair and continued with my questioning.

'How was the property passed from mother to daughter? Since it seems that all the children, except me have been illegitimate?'

Harriet moved some papers around on her desk until she unearthed a pen and wrote on one of the documents she had just printed.

'They got around the property laws of the time, by the mother selling the property to the daughter. The unfortunate rift between Vivienne and Vera has isolated you from a very important connection to the past. However, my dear, it is my firm belief that you have the strength to forge your own path, unhindered by some of the stranger, ingrained misconceptions carried by your grandmother for instance.'

'Such as?' I asked.

Harriet pushed the documents in my direction and indicated where she wanted me to sign. I picked them up and began reading.

Harriet said, 'Well, none of the women married. And I know for a fact, that Vivienne followed this rule blindly, even though she had fallen deeply in love with Vera's father.'

I paused in my reading and asked, 'Did you know my grandfather?'

'No. That was just one of the many secrets that she took to her grave. I cannot help you with anything except legal matters and probably give you some unwanted personal observations on your grandmother.'

I smiled at that comment, she had obviously read *my* micro expressions very well. After signing all the required documentation, I thanked Harriet and left.

Hungry after my long morning with that fierce old woman, I needed food and went in search of a café.

Harriet had more in common with my grandmother than she believed. 'Cut from the same cloth,' was the expression Mum would have used. She was right about one thing - I did have to forge my own path. What I found curious, was that I wanted to.

Even though my encounters with the dead were scary, especially the manner of their passing, I knew I had found my calling in life.

Other concerns hovered in the background of my mind.

What about a child?

Would I be able to have a baby?

Robert and I had not managed to fall pregnant.

And George, was it possible I was falling in love?

CHAPTER TWENTY-TWO

Winter's frosty breath had turned the dew on the ground to a thin layer of ice. Despite wearing a thick coat, scarf, beanie, gloves, and woollen socks, I shivered as the arctic air seeped through to the inner layers of my clothing.

Apparently impervious to the cold, Chance ran ahead of me as I made my way to the bails. Though autumn had passed without another visitor, I no longer bought milk from the supermarket. My boots left a wet trail in the grass as I walked across to where Lavender and Beetle waited for me.

Surreptitiously, I glanced around, I couldn't see her, but I knew she was watching. For the past several days, I had felt Dardanelle's eyes on me as I went about my daily chores. Often, at the edge of my sight I caught a wisp of a shadow, or a white haze.

The ghost's constant presence had become unsettling.

Eager to be relieved of the fullness in her udder, Lavender trotted into the bails and began licking at the molasses I had prepared for her. Removing my gloves, I cleaned her udder and lay my forehead against her warm flank, grateful for the heat radiating from her large body.

Gently, I began to massage her swollen teats, drawing out the creamy milk and watching it flow into the pail resting on the ground between my knees. Beside me, Chance waited, in his usual impatient manner, for his daily serving. When I finished, I placed a small amount of milk in a saucer for him and he lapped contentedly.

It didn't surprise me when Chance growled quietly; he didn't stop drinking, which meant he was aware she was close, but not bothered. I tugged at the kick rope, releasing Lavender's leg and liberated her neck from the head stall. She backed away, mooing gently to Beetle who, when I opened the gate, rushed out of her pen. Tail wagging in anticipation, the calf butted her mother's flank, then sucked hungrily on her teat.

'What do you want, Dardanelle?'

I'd asked this question before and never received an answer, but she had chosen to reveal herself and now stood close to the railings.

Not wanting to give her too much of my attention, I didn't look at her. I unwound the hose and turned the tap on to wash away the manure and debris from the floor of the bails.

'You are different to the others. Not all could see, hear, and speak.'

'That's a bit cryptic. What do you mean by that?'

'The old woman before you, she could hear but did not listen.'

I shrugged, glanced at her briefly, then concentrated on cleaning. 'A lot of people are like that. Why have you been following me? What is it you want?'

'You love this man who comes to visit you? The one called George.'

The question took me by surprise. I stopped and stared at her, and perhaps for the first time, saw her not as a ghost, but as another woman. Unsettled, I returned to the task at hand without answering.

The cleaning finished, milk pail in hand, I made my way towards the house. Dardanelle was perceptive in her question regarding George. I'd asked myself the same question many times over the last couple of months.

For George and me, going to the movies and having dinner afterwards had become a weekly event. On weekends, we gathered up our backpacks and with his dogs for company, we hiked along various trails. Occasionally, we held hands, more often we walked beside each other in contented silence. The connection between us was growing into something that I didn't want to explore just yet, and George, bless him for his finely tuned intuition, was giving me space, allowing me to set the pace of our relationship. His presence in my life had restored something I thought I'd lost, or perhaps never had – a sense of belonging.

Dardanelle's voice interrupted my reverie, 'Your silence tells me you do. Be careful, men are driven by desire and lie if they do not get what they want.'

'This is as far as you can come.' I told her as we came closer to the house.

'I wait. You come. I wish to talk.'

This was such a sharp contrast from her usual defiant attitude, I stopped then and turned to look at her. I couldn't quite define the change I saw in her. A calmness perhaps. I wasn't sure, but some of the tension, that I usually felt when she was around, seeped out of me. I studied her through narrowed eyes, not sure whether to trust the change I sensed.

'What's changed, Dardanelle? You seem different.'

'Not me. You.'

'Me? I'm still the same, I haven't changed.'

'No. I change because I watch you. I tell you this before. You are different to the others. They chase me away. They are frightened, I think now.'

'You have a lot of anger in you, Dardanelle. People are often fearful when they sense anger in others.'

Especially ghosts. I thought but didn't say, then added. 'Not only that, did you lure any of their visitors away?'

Her eyes flashed with sudden anger. 'You do not understand! I am alone, and I take no-one who does not want to come with me.'

We held each other's gaze for several long moments, before she visibly forced herself to relax. I took a deep breath and released some of my own tension.

'I have things to do. I'll come later,' I told her, walking away.

This was a woman or ghost who, I felt, had to be kept firmly at arm's length. At least, I understood her a little better.

A lonely ghost - who would have thought?

I didn't look back until I reached the verandah.

She was gone.

CHAPTER TWENTY-THREE

'Why do you not come to me?' Dardanelle asked two days later.

She hovered at the edge of the garden, watching me remove weeds. I stood and stretched my aching back. If it hadn't been for Fred's prolonged stay, I wouldn't have considered making a garden. Growing my own vegetables was not something I had ever been interested in, not when there was a perfectly good supermarket at my disposal.

'I suppose it's because I don't trust you.' I told her.

Reaching for the shovel, I began to turn over the soil. With spring on its way, it was time to decide what to plant, but before I could do that, I needed to prepare the ground.

'I wish to talk. That is all.' There was a hurt, sulkiness in her voice.

I stopped my digging and looked at her. Usually, all I could see was a hazy shape, but now that figure was clearer, as were the details of her form.

Dardanelle was younger than I'd first thought. Hurt, hazel eyes returned my gaze. Long, light brown, curly hair held in place by a grubby ribbon, framed a heart shaped face. In life, she would have been beautiful. Her feet were bare, and her clothes ragged looking; had they been my clothes, they would have found their way to the bin before now.

A rush of pity touched me. Determined not to let it show, I said, 'Talk then and I will listen.'

I returned to digging the earth.

'Look at me. Let me know you see me,' she insisted, though I heard a plea as well.

With a sigh, I stopped digging, pushed the shovel into the ground and said, 'Come with me.'

I led her over to the fallen log in the orchard. She sat on one end and I on the other. Chance joined us and positioned himself between us in the middle of the log.

'He protects you.'

'He does.' I told her.

Dardanelle began and I sat in silence and listened as she freed the story, she had held too close for too long.

'When I am fifteen, I go into service for a vicar with a wife and many children. It is a good life, and I am happy. I am there, maybe a year, and a new man joins the parish. When he sees me ...,' she paused, and I wait, the pain in her voice is clear. Haltingly, she begins again. 'He wants me, for his wife, he says. The vicar tells him I am too young, and he must wait. Each year he asks. But I no want this man and tell the vicar. The man, he becomes angry. He said I steal. I do not steal, but he say this because I do not want his affection. I spurn him ... so he lies, and I am sent to this brown country.'

'Who was he? Why did they believe him and not you?'

'He is believed because he has money, and he is a man.' She spat the words out. 'And I ... I am just a woman.'

Barely a woman, I think but do not say, instead I ask. 'What about the vicar? Did he believe you?'

'Yes. But this man is an important man. He is rich.' Anger and hurt rule the tone in her voice, though many years had passed since these events took place.

I hold a deep breath and let it out slowly. High in the sky, a hawk flew lazy circles. Dardanelle was quiet, and for a time we watched the hunter together, riding the air currents, in search of its next meal.

When she continued, the anger had gone from her voice, it had been replaced by apprehension. 'When I leave the ship, I am given to a man to work in his house ... a housekeeper he tells me. And for a time, all is peace. This man has no interest in me. He has a beautiful garden, and when he not work, he tends his garden. It has many beautiful shrubs with flowers, and a large shady tree at the back.'

She paused, and I looked over at her. Dardanelle's hands had formed fists and were clutching at her worn out skirt. Her face was distorted by strong emotions. I waited in silence and watched as she brought them under control.

'One day, the master tells me he has letter from his brothers, and they will join us from the old country. He is not happy. I can see this, and I begin to worry about these three brothers who are coming.' Her voice faded; she appeared to be lost in the memory of that time.

Dardanelle's tone was strained with tension when she picked up her story, 'They come these three brothers, and I ... I am one woman.' Her voice broke with a barely controlled sob, then dropped to a whisper.

What her words implied, filled me with nausea. Not knowing what to say, I said nothing.

'Soon, I am with child.'

I nod as I struggle to hold back tears.

'One day, the master shows me a bush in the garden. It has bright yellow flowers. He tells me he will be staying in town; I am to pick ten leaves from this bush and add them to the stew I must make for the brothers while he is away. He tells me, I must not eat this meal I make.'

Nearing midday, the sun was making its way towards its zenith. The frost had melted, and the birds were finding places where they could sunbathe and warm up.

Chance moved gracefully and silently off the log, he shifted effortlessly to a hunting crouch and glided his way towards a pair of birds laying on the ground, sunning themselves.

I watched his silent passage and listened to Dardanelle's history with a sense of foreboding that settled in my solar plexus like a heavy rock.

'The brothers, they eat this meal that I make, and they become ill, very ill, and I am frightened. I run to the neighbours to tell them to get the master and a doctor. But they are too late and the brothers ...,' her voice falters before she continues, 'they die.'

Unaware that I'd held my breath, I gasped, pulling a sudden rush of air into my lungs. Chance, preparing to launch himself at the unsuspecting birds, looked back at me suddenly. His gaze swept across me to Dardanelle, who he eyed suspiciously. His movement triggered an alarm in the birds, and they flew off. Chance gave me an exasperated look, as if accusing me of losing him his prey, then sat and cleaned his paws.

At the other end of the log, Dardanelle had fallen silent. She appeared to be looking at the scene before us, though whether she saw it or not, I couldn't tell. The silence dragged on for so long I thought she had finished speaking.

She gave an audible gulp, and said softly, 'Soon my master brings boys home at night. They eat the meal I make, then they go into his room. This happens many times but one boy ... he fights. I hear screams, and in the morning, the master, he ...,' I wait in tense silence. 'He tells me, I must dig big hole in the garden.'

Dardanelle paused, her image shook as if she was taking one long shuddering breath, before continuing.

'I dig this hole where he shows me, and when it is night. The boy, we bury him.'

Nothing in my life had prepared me for the dreadful story Dardanelle was describing. There was too much pain and sadness in her voice for me to doubt the veracity of her words.

Her voice dropped to a whisper, and I strained to hear her. 'We stand beside the boy's grave, and the master, he says, 'If that child you carry is a girl, it will join this boy. If it is a boy child, then I will have a use for him.' I am sick at his words. I have much fear inside of me for my child ... and for me.'

My brain was numb with horror. A quick glance at Dardanelle's face showed a young woman reliving a nightmare. I waited in silence for her to find the fortitude to finish what she wanted to tell me.

'For many days, I don't know what to do, but soon I know what I must do. A day comes when the master is away. I take the ladder, I have rope, and I climb the beautiful tree in the back. My belly is heavy with child, and it is hard, but I know I do this for my baby. I sit for ... a long time. It is so beautiful. I have come to love this brown land. The birds, they come visit me and watch. They know, I think, what I am going to do. They sing, and I am calm. I must save my child from the master. With the rope around my neck, I jump.'

When the tears started, I had no idea. They poured unheeded down my face and neck. Once I became aware of their presence, I wiped my face on my sleeves. Had she been in the flesh I would have hugged her, but all I could do was cry, and I had no words of comfort for the girl wraith who sat on the other end of the log.

CHAPTER TWENTY-FOUR

In the following days, the pain of Dardanelle's story filled my waking hours and my nights as well. I dreamt of a young girl tying one end of a rope around a strong branch and the other around her own neck, before launching herself off into space in order to snap her neck: all in an effort to save her unborn baby from a life of depravity.

After I had wiped away the tears, I turned to Dardanelle, and we held each other's gaze for several long minutes. It felt as if time stood still, our souls met, connected, and drew slowly apart until at last we were two again.

Her smile was soft and barely touched her lips, but her eyes shone with goodwill for the first time since I first saw her.

'You see me now?' she asked hopefully.

'I see you,' I replied, doing my best to hold back a fresh lot of tears.

I sat on my end of the log long after her departure. My unseeing gaze rested on the landscape before me, but all I saw, were the pictures, created by Dardanelle's words, in my head,

'That's the first time she's told that story.' Rupert's voice interrupted the images in my mind.

I became aware of Chance's warm body curled around my feet. The sun lay suspended not far above the western horizon. My stomach growled with hunger, my backside was numb, and I was stiff from sitting for so long. I eased Chance out of the way, stood and stretched, before turning towards Rupert.

He had taken Dardanelle's place on the other end of the log. Smoke curled from the bowl of his pipe; he had obviously been sitting there a while before he spoke.

'Why now, do you think? She's been dead a long time.' I queried.

'Early to mid-eighteen hundreds, I believe,' he told me, puffing contentedly on his pipe.

'Did you know?'

There was a touch of something, exasperation perhaps, in his gaze. He removed the pipe from between his teeth, and replied, 'I don't know *everything*, child.'

Child, there he goes again.

Annoyance swept through me at his words, but then I figured to him I was a child.

'I understand her a little better now,' I told him, regaining my seat on the log.

Chance bit me on the ankle to let me know he was sick of sitting in the cold, when we could be inside a warm house. I rubbed my hand along his back, and he arched in response.

'Soon,' I murmured, and he resettled at my feet.

'Perhaps she wanted to be understood,' Rupert told me, then added. 'Though she has never given anyone else the opportunity. She always checks out the newcomers. Some, more than others, she has stayed to provoke. She has driven many a guardian to distraction and has led more than one soul astray.'

'Has she always been here? On this property, I mean.'

'No. Maybe a hundred years in time as you know it.'

'What happened to them? The souls she enticed away I mean.'

The old man shrugged, 'I know some were recovered, but not all. It is not for me to know.'

'Why now? Why me do you think?'

'I would say it is because you have a familiar, and she sees that as a powerful sign.'

'He is a cat, Rupert. A cat!'

'Be that as it may. You have only begun your journey, who knows what lies ahead of you. She is right, you are not like the others. Perhaps she thinks you are able to do something for her that the others could not ... or would not.'

'Well, I don't know what that could be.'

'Think about it. You will find the answer.'

With that unhelpful remark, Rupert tapped his pipe gently on the log, stood and in two short steps, he disappeared.

'Vanishing like that is a very bad habit, old man.' I yelled.

CHAPTER TWENTY-FIVE

George sat at my kitchen table, watching me count cups of flour into a bowl. Reluctantly, I'd added making bread to the list of things that I needed to learn. Self-sufficiency was all very well if that was what you wanted to do, but when it was foisted on you, there was a certain amount of gritting of teeth required.

'Have you seen her since?' He asked after I had told him of my recent encounter with Dardanelle.

I shook my head and frowned at him, 'Six. No. Let me finish this.'

Glancing at the recipe again, I finished assembling the dry mixture before replying. 'I haven't seen her. Well, not completely. She's hovering again, so obviously she is making up her mind about something.'

Picking up a jug, I measured warm water, added yeast, honey, and oil, mixing them all together before adding the mix to the dry ingredients.

'I think she might be ready to pass on,' I told George, blending all the ingredients together. 'I also think for the time being we should suspend our outings. I want to be here if she ...,'

'You have a life to live too.' George interrupted, the tension in his voice made me stop mid stir and look at him.

Stiffness carved every line of his face into deeper furrows. Anger blazed in his dark eyes but hurt hovered behind the wrath.

'Or is this just an excuse not to see ...,'

'George!' I snapped, stopping him mid-sentence.

He pushed back his chair and stood so that I had to look up at him. He was a tall man, made even taller by my shorter stature.

'Don't you 'George' me woman, I thought we had ... have something special, and I'm not going to let some bloody ...,' he stopped, spluttered, 'ghost come between us.'

Bread making forgotten, I stood facing him with my hands on my hips and my face feeling redder by the second.

'And what if you had a cow that was having trouble giving birth?' I asked, doing my best to keep an even tone. 'Or a machine that had broken down in the middle of something important or ...,' I finished lamely, since I had no idea what he used his machines for.

'You're comparing the birth of a calf to ... to,' he stopped, and comprehension appeared in his eyes, before he barked a short laugh. 'Oh! I see. The calf is coming, and she is ... you think she is going or wanting to go.'

He rocked back on his heels for a moment, nodding his head. I could see him turning the idea over in his mind.

If I hadn't been so mad at him, I might have kissed him.

Instead, I said. 'So, finally you get it. Took you long enough,' I told him, knowing that he had actually got 'it' pretty darn quick.

I kept my hands on my hips and glared at him. George studied me with a softer, but unsure look in his eyes.

'So, we're good?'

We held each other's gaze for several long seconds as the anger seeped out of me and was replaced by a sudden shyness that I hadn't felt since - forever. I felt a blush touch by cheeks and quickly turned away to avoid his eyes and occupy myself with turning the dough out onto a floured table.

George sat and I glanced at him out of the corner of my eye. A knowing grin touched his lips, and he murmured softly, 'Oh, we're good.'

CHAPTER TWENTY-SIX

In order to work out some repressed frustration, and fill the empty wood box as well, I swung the axe above my head, then smashed it down onto the block of wood, splitting it in two.

George knew what he wanted. I knew what George wanted, and I was fairly sure I wanted the same thing; the question was - did I want it now? Was I ready for a more intimate relationship? How would it all work? Maybe there was a good reason all my ancestors had chosen to remain single? How could I fit in a relationship with George around the dead?

If not now, when? A small voice in the back of head replied. *Shut up*, I told it silently and swung the axe again, only harder this time.

Ever since I had embarrassed myself by blushing like a shy teenager on her first date; I'd avoided George and given him the brush off on more than one occasion, sometimes not very politely. A mental image of that small knowing grin touching those rather kissable lips had me swinging the axe even harder.

'You trying to split the log on top, or the one underneath?' said the source of my frustration.

Surprise stopped me mid swing, and I frowned at my visitor.

'Go away George,' I said, finishing the swing. To hold it out of harm's way, I slammed the axe into the chopping block instead.

Turning my back on George, I picked up the pieces of wood I'd cut and added them to the basket.

'Would you like a cold drink or a cup of tea?' He asked, ignoring my rudeness.

'Shouldn't that be my question?'

'Yes, but were you going to ask it?'

'No. I want you to leave.' I told him, attempting to pick up the basket of firewood that I had overfilled, making it too heavy for me to carry.

George stopped me as I went to empty some of the wood from the container. Gripping the handles, he carried the overburdened basket towards the house.

Bloody man!

I gritted my teeth in vexation and followed.

Inside, George placed the container on the floor. Methodically, he transferred the wood from the basket to the wood-box. I watched him for one long irritating moment before leaving him to it.

In the bathroom, hoping to regain some composure, I lingered over washing my hands and face.

Knowing my behaviour was childish and changing it, was an entirely different thing. Taking a deep breath, I went back to the kitchen.

George had the kettle going and was taking a mug (for me) and a teacup (for him) out of the cupboard. He knew me too well. I drank tea but not very often, and he only drank one cup of coffee a day, and that was first thing in the morning.

He looked up at my approach, 'I came to talk. And, if we're going to make a go of this, to clear the air. That's all.'

I nodded and nudged him towards a chair. The first thing I needed to do, was to take control of my own kitchen.

'Look George,' I said as I turned away, and began to remove tea leaves and coffee grounds from the cupboard.

'No. Wait. Let me start,' he insisted, not sitting, 'I've just come to say, I know you're not ready and I'll wait.'

'What if I'm never ready? Anyway, it's not that I'm not ready. It's just that ... what if I'm just being a coward?' I asked.

Concentrating on placing tea leaves in the tea pot and coffee in the plunger, gave me an excuse not to look at him – so much for taking control.

He chuckled. 'One thing you are not, and that is a coward.'

'How do you figure that?' I looked up in surprise and faced him.

With his head at an angle and a tender look in his eye, he said, 'You jumped into a creek to save a drowning cat, and you deal with the dead. How many people do you think would be able to do what you do?'

'Anyone else would do the same thing,' I told him. 'And anyway, there are different types of cowardice. Just because someone can, say run into a burning building, or jump into a river and almost drown, doesn't mean they'll be able to be honest and giving and loving to someone they ... love.' I gulped and my voice faltered, worried I'd said too much.

George studied me for a moment before moving to the fridge. Taking out the milk and cream, he placed them on the table.

I grimaced; it seemed making afternoon tea had become a two-person job.

'You're right,' he told me. 'Of course, you're right. There are different types of cowardice but none of that applies to you.'

'What if it doesn't work out? How would it work? With you and the dead? What happens then? I will still need your support here. I don't want to give this up, George. And what about children? You want children, I know you do. And I'm not sure I can have children. Robert and I tried, and well ... it never happened, and neither of us could be bothered finding out the reason why we couldn't have children. In fact, I think we were both relieved.'

Now, I was following him around the kitchen, talking to his back. When had this become a dance?

Removing the boiling kettle from the stove, George added water to the teapot and the coffee plunger. 'I thought that might be part of the problem. And I do want children, but I want you first and if children come later, well that'll be the 'icing on the cake,' as the saying goes.' he said.

George returned the kettle to a cooler part of the stove, and we sat and waited in silence for the beverages to steep. Our gazes held and our breathing harmonised. A bubble formed around us, there was just the two of us, suspended in time, communicating without words.

Until Chance jumped on the table, moved between us, and swatted me on the nose. I blinked and the moment passed.

Seemingly content with his intervention, Chance left the table and sauntered outside.

Bloody cat!

A reflective harmony connected us as George and I sipped at our respective beverages, allowing a quiet settling of emotions. Occasionally I glanced at George, to see him look quickly away.

George placed his teacup in the saucer with a rattle, I glanced at him in surprise at the sudden noise.

'Children are a long way away, but I promise you,' he told me, inhaling deeply then letting the air out through his nose in a rush, 'if what we have between us doesn't work, nothing will change. I will help you no matter what.'

He stood then, and taking my hands drew me up from my seat. 'But more than anything in the world, I want to give this, us … a go. It's too important, not to. I've never felt like this about anyone else.'

Our eyes met, held, and I was sure the longing I saw in his eyes was reflected in mine. There was no doubt in his, but I was pretty sure that along with yearning, he would see confusion and uncertainty in mine.

George drew me into his arms, held me for several heartbeats then placing his hands on my shoulder, he gently pushed me away.

I stepped back into his arms and held him close. I didn't want to let him go, so why was I filled with so much doubt?

Holding me firmly but tenderly he said, 'When you are ready, you come to me.'

Pushing me away so that he could look into my eyes, he gave me a little shake as if to emphasise his words. 'In the meantime, I will check in occasionally and if ever you need me, you only have to ask.'

'Okay?' He asked, giving me another not so gentle shake.

I managed to nod between shakes that also waggled my head.

George seemed to be able to discern the nods I was contributing to the nods he was eliciting. 'Good,' he said.

After another long appraisal of me, following which he, apparently satisfied, turned then, and walked out the door.

I was left asking myself why I was such a darn, cowardly fool and why couldn't I, just for once, jump in with both feet. I could do that to save a bloody cat, but not for my own happiness.

Maybe that was the problem. I couldn't be sure that I would be happy.

CHAPTER TWENTY-SEVEN

Dardanelle sat cross-legged on the ground, watching me weed and water the garden I had planted. A stiff breeze tugged at my hat and clothes. As if she were a painting on a canvas propped up against the tree she sat under, her long hair and raggedy clothes remained untouched by the wind. Her eyes were downcast, though every now and then, she flicked them in my direction. She had something to say, but I was not going to try to draw it out of her. She would have to tell me in her own time.

Chance lay watching us from the other end of the garden beds. He no longer spat and hissed every time Dardanelle appeared; but he never relaxed until she was gone.

Winter had relaxed its icy grip on the climate and the promise of spring floated on the cool air. Deciding to keep it simple, I had planted potatoes, sweet potatoes, and pumpkin; nourishing vegetables I figured the possums wouldn't be too interested in eating. Seeds, from some old tomatoes I had thrown in with the hens, had taken hold. Initially, I had transferred the seedlings to pots, in time I thought I would transfer them back to the earth.

Hopefully, none of my visitors would stay longer than a few weeks, and the food I produced would last until their transition.

George kept his word I hadn't seen him for a couple of weeks. My heart ached with missing him, but I was determined to be sure it was what I wanted, and not some passing fancy, before I jumped into that particular fire.

I was in the process of kneeling, in order to reach across and pull out a weed, when Dardanelle spoke at last, though the question took me by surprise.

'Do you think me evil?'

Mid kneel, I fell backwards onto my bottom and stared at her in disbelief.

'Evil! Good heavens, No. Why would I think that?'

'It is evil to kill. This is what the good book says.' Dardanelle's eyes were filled with fear and worry. 'I will go to hell.'

Weeding forgotten, I wrenched off my gumboots, and mimicked Dardanelle by sitting cross-legged on the ground. Plucking a long-stemmed piece of grass, I placed it in my mouth and chewed on its stalk. It gave me time to think on her words. Whatever I thought she would say, it was never that.

I wasn't sure what to say, but I had to start somewhere, so I asked, 'Did you know the three brothers would die?'

'NO!' said Dardanelle, horrified. 'I ... I want these men to die, but I do not want to *kill* them!'

Of course she wanted them to die. I would have wanted them to die too. Whether or not I would have killed them had I been in her place, was something best left unexplored. Somehow, I had to get her to acknowledge that she was not the one responsible for their deaths.

'Your master knew they would die, didn't he?'

She nodded, her eyes not meeting mine. Dardanelle's hands made plucking motions at the grass, though her fingers were unable to make contact.

'I cannot touch,' she whimpered. 'I am nothing.' There were tears in the sound of her voice if not her eyes.

There was nothing I could say, so I changed the subject.

'Do you think you may be carrying a burden that is not your own?'

'What you mean by this? The master he say, I make meal. I add leaves. I kill the brothers. He tells me it is my fault. How can you not understand this?' Her tone left me in no doubt that, in her mind, she had added - *Are you stupid?*

I sighed. 'Dardanelle, if you told me to do something that you knew would kill someone, but I did not. Who would be responsible? You or me?'

She mulled this over in her mind for quite a while before I saw a glimmer of understanding light her eyes. Almost immediately, the light flickered out and she said, 'I kill my baby. I kill myself. They bury me outside the church. It is grave sin. I go to hell.'

In sudden understanding, I watched her in silence, then said, 'Killing yourself is no longer seen as a sin, Dardanelle. People who kill themselves are buried in consecrated grounds these days. And it seems to me, that you killed yourself in order to save your baby. Isn't that, right?'

Abruptly she stood. 'You have answer for everything. But it is I who will burn in the fires of hell. Not you! You ... Witch! You know nothing!' She yelled, before disappearing.

Bloody ghosts and their disappearing acts.

I flopped back onto the grass. Above me, fluffy white clouds drifted across a pastel blue sky, here and there streaky hints of cobalt added a deeper splash of colour. The breeze had settled and now wafted gently across my face. Birds called noisily to each other. The sun sat halfway towards midday. Above me, all was peace, but I was tired, worn out by my emotions and the emotions of others.

Two hundred years of worrying she would burn in hell had kept Dardanelle's spirit roaming the earth. Until she let go of her fears she would continue to roam. As much as I wanted to help, unless her thoughts about her situation changed, there was nothing I could do.

And bloody George, what was I going to do about him? I wanted to feel his arms around me and his warm body on mine. Ghosts were a poor substitute for a flesh and blood relationship.

Chance came over and sniffed me, climbed onto my abdomen, curled up and went to sleep. He always had the best ideas. We lay like this for a while before my eyes slowly closed and I too, slept.

CHAPTER TWENTY-EIGHT

The sun had reached its summit and was descending westwards, when I woke to Chance growling, and a now familiar unnatural cold.

Immediately, I knew I had another visitor.

I eased Chance off my belly, sat up and looked around, whoever the visitor was, he or she was not close by. I sighed, gained my feet, brushed leaves, and twigs from my clothes, then, in search of our new arrival, Chance and I made our way towards the house.

My foot had barely touched the first step on the stairs leading to the back verandah, when a soft mewling whimper had the hairs on the back of my neck standing to attention. A dread feeling crept into the pit of my stomach and rose to the vicinity of my heart. My breath caught, held and I paused to make myself take a few steadying breaths.

The sounds told me my visitor was a child.

I found her on the front verandah in the same spot I had found John. In her cries, I heard pain and terror. At the sight of her, my stomach clenched, and I felt sick.

She lay naked and curled into a foetal position on the bare verandah floorboards. Bruises encircled her neck like a dirty necklace. Other, larger bruises covered her ribs and hips. Dried rivulets of blood clung to her inner thighs, telling a story so horrific, sudden tears stung my eyes. I brushed them away. There would be time enough for tears later.

Gathering her into my arms, I carried the little girl into the house and wrapped her in a blanket I grabbed off the bed in the spare bedroom. In front of the warm stove, I sat with her curled on my lap.

It was a long time before her body stopped shaking and heaving. Her thumb crept into her mouth, and finally she slept.

The child whimpered softly in her sleep, as I gently wiped the dirt and blood from her tiny body. Dressed in one of my t-shirts, I laid her on my bed and covered her with warm blankets.

Chance jumped on the bed and lay beside her, as if on guard. I watched them for several minutes, before convincing myself that she was not going to wake, and I was free to leave her. If she did wake, Chance would warn me.

Rummaging around in the wardrobe in the spare bedroom, I searched for articles of clothing that I thought would fit the wounded child sleeping in my bed.

Guided by some deeper instinct, I had cleaned the clothes when I first arrived, not knowing nor understanding the use that they served. As I laid out the small outfits and sorted through them, I realised that they told their own stories. I saw them through changed eyes and handled them with a reverence I had not felt before.

The clothes had been worn and washed many times. When I had a chance, I would buy clothing that suited a child of today. In the meantime, I chose garments that I thought would fit and be comfortable.

For two days the little girl slept. I was loathe to leave the house, but Lavender needed milking and the garden attending, even if the weeds could be left to grow wild for the time being.

Chance rarely left her side. I grew more relaxed as I went about my day knowing that, should I be needed, he would let me know. I had no doubt that by now, George would know that I had a visitor. He'd told me the property became shrouded when I had a visitor, though I wished I could contact him to find out more about the little girl. She had obviously died in terrible circumstances, and I knew that once she woke, I would not be asking her any questions.

Her sleep seemed as deep as ever as I watched her. I hadn't collected the newspaper the day she arrived, neither had I been down to check for others since her arrival.

'Stay with her Chance,' I told him. 'I'm going to check the mailbox.'

He gave me a side eyed glance and grumbled something deep in his chest. I took it to be an agreement, or maybe it was something I was better off not knowing.

Leaving Chance in charge, I walked down to the mailbox. Only one newspaper waited for me.

Back at the house, I made a coffee and sat at the table on the back verandah; and settled down to check the newspaper for any news of the child sleeping in my bedroom.

What I found stunned me. A picture of my visitor, with a report that a massive search had been instigated for eight-year-old Lily Smithson, who had wandered away from a family picnic. It was dated the day before Lily appeared at the house.

I was rereading the story when Chance jumped up on the table and sat on the newspaper.

'OH! Oh! Lily you're awake.'

Absorbed by the obvious inaccuracies in the article I was reading, I hadn't heard her approach. Thumb in mouth, with an intently wary but curious expression on her face, she stood beside me.

Taking her thumb out of her mouth, she asked, 'What's your name?'

'Sandrine, but you can call me Sandy,' I told her.

Lily nodded, then pointing at Chance, she added, 'What's his name?'

She grinned around the thumb she had replaced in her mouth, when I told her, as if the name met with her approval.

'Come with me and we'll find some clothes for you to wear.'

I held out my hand. Lily shook her head in refusal. I led the way, with Chance at my heels. She followed me or maybe him, into the spare bedroom where she chose the clothes she wanted to wear.

The following days passed with a heavy quiet enveloping the house. Lily picked at her food but loved drinking hot chocolate. I felt completely out of my depth. I had been a community nurse, and had little experience with children, and certainly none with traumatised children. I watched the dwindling supply of chocolate with something akin to panic. What was I going to do when it ran out? More to the point, what would Lily do when I could no longer supply her with what I thought was her comfort food?

With a lot of encouragement, Lily followed me down to the mailbox, to leave a note for George. I hoped that he would not only find the note but be able to replenish my supplies of drinking chocolate. I wasn't sure that things *could* be passed back and forth between us. Leaving notes for George was something I had never tried before, but if she stayed much longer then I would run out of the chocolate she loved so much.

Exercise and fresh air became the reason for the daily excursion to the front gate and an excuse for both Lily and I to escape the confines of the house.

As the days passed no more newspapers came. My unclaimed note to George remained in the mailbox. It became clear that the energy field around the property prevented any exchange of information.

Retrieving the note, I prayed that Lily would take the loss of her favourite drink, calmly.

CHAPTER TWENTY-NINE

Spring's arrival had parent birds gathering food for their new off-spring's voracious appetites. Flowers, dormant during winter, provided a variety of colour to the now greener landscape.

Lavender was determinedly making attempts to wean Beetle, though the calf still sometimes bullied her mother into allowing her to suck. I continued to lock Beetle up at night in order to obtain enough milk for us to drink.

Lily appeared content with warm milk and honey in lieu of hot chocolate, and I had stopped worrying about how to interact with her. I couldn't decide whether her quiet manner and remarkable self-containment was her usual personality, or the result of her trauma.

Our days slipped into a familiar routine of milking, gardening, and housework. Chance followed me and Lily followed Chance. Occasionally, he would hide, and she would search the house and grounds for him; when she was almost ready to admit defeat, he would pop out of his hiding place and grab her ankles. Her screams were filled with a combination of glee, fright, and exasperation that once again Chance had tricked her.

At other times I would find her hiding. Her large blue eyes staring with horror at something only she could see. During these times, Chance would settle down beside her and wait until the terror within her subsided. Then she would creep out and come to me to be held. We would sit until she left my lap to wander outside among the trees. Chance shadowed her, and I watched their meandering from the verandah.

A month after Lily's arrival, morning dawned with a fine mist covering the countryside. The birds were making their early sunrise calls to each other. Lily skipped down to the bails with Chance, and I tagged along behind. Lavender greeted me with a soft moo and walked into the bails for her morning molasses. Securing the head stall and leg rope, I sat with my head against her warm flank to milk her.

I was almost finished when Lily, with her thumb in her mouth, came to stand beside me.

'What's wrong?' I said, lifting my head in surprise. She had stopped sucking her thumb. It crept back into her mouth when she was apprehensive or uncertain.

'There's someone here.' Lily whispered, staring at something behind me.

Normally, she perched on the railings and watched me as I milked Lavender.

Chance, intent on receiving his daily quota of milk, appeared unconcerned by the newcomer. I shifted on the block of wood I used as a seat and turned to see Dardanelle staring intently at Lily.

'This is Lily, Dardanelle. Don't frighten her.'

'I will not,' breathed Dardanelle. 'She is so beautiful. Can I talk to you child?' Dardanelle had not even glanced at me; all her attention was on Lily.

Lily looked to me for reassurance. When I nodded, she approached Dardanelle shyly; they stared at each other in silence for several moments. I watched them communicate wordlessly before turning back to Lavender. By the time I had finished the milking and cleaned the bails, Lily had followed Dardanelle into the orchard.

Chance sat beside me as we contemplated them for several long moments. Not feeling any sense of unease, Chance and I left them and returned to the house.

The following morning, I woke to a child's happy laughter. The feeling of heaviness that I had carried with me since Lily's arrival, but had been unaware of until then, lifted. Following the delightful sound to the back of the house, I peeked through the kitchen window. Lily sat on the steps, while Dardanelle entertained her with wild dancing, cartwheels, and handstands.

'Teach me, Nellie,' she yelled, leaping from the steps and running across to Dardanelle. Lily danced around her shouting. 'Teach me. Teach me.'

'I like that name you give me. I am Nellie now,' the Wraith cried joyfully, spinning around and around.

So begun a change in the routine of our days. The girls chased each other through the paddocks, played hide and seek, and danced around trees. Lily adorned her hair with flowers, and didn't understand when she couldn't do the same to Dardanelle's hair. It didn't stop her from continuing to try.

'Why won't the flowers stay in your hair?' Her question tugged at my heart. I knew how much Dardanelle would have loved the feel of ... anything. The joy of having the beauty of flowers in her hair would have overwhelmed her.

Sometimes, Chance joined them in their game of hide and seek and often ruined their entertainment by finding the one who was hiding. More than once I heard, 'Naughty Chance.'

I listened to their laughter, watched them play, and went about my chores; marvelling at, and grateful for the connection they had formed with each other. Dardanelle's presence had not only wrought an important change in Lily; she'd softened, and I could see a blossoming occurring within her.

Now that I wasn't so occupied with Lily, my thoughts turned often to George.

Was he thinking of me as much as I was thinking of him?

Was he well?

Could we make it work?

Other times, I would find myself staring in the direction of his property. Wanting to see him and touch him so much, the pain of it felt physical. I hadn't consciously acknowledged the decision I had made; it hovered in the forefront of my mind waiting to catch me unaware.

CHAPTER THIRTY

'Sandy?' The question in Lily's voice stopped me, mid wipe of the dish I had in my hand, to look at her. Lost in my thoughts of George, I hadn't noticed the lull in the sounds of the girls' voices. Used to their occasional silence, I'd paid no heed to it.

'I want Nellie to sleep with me. Please Sandy please. She said she's not allowed in the house, but I want her to sleep with me. She's my friend.'

I studied her pleading little face for a moment.

'Is this your idea or Dar ... Nellie's?'

'It's mine.' There was no hesitation in her reply, so I accepted it as truth.

'And where would you both sleep?' I asked since Lily, Chance and I continued to share my bed.

'In the bed ... in the other room?' She replied hesitantly.

My lips twitched to stop from smiling. She, or they, had certainly thought about it a lot. I looked out the window to see Dardanelle waiting and watching with a hopeful expression in her eyes.

'Let me think about it and I will let you know by the end of the day. Okay.'

Lily's arrival had solidified the changes I had watched take place slowly in Dardanelle. The angry, fierce woman I first met had disappeared, and now I saw the young girl that she really was.

I spent the rest of the day mulling my answer over in my mind and could find no reason to say no, though there would have to be restrictions. I went in search of the girls to tell them of my decision, and the limitations that would have to be agreed on.

Afternoon shadows were lengthening. A cool breeze had removed the heat from the day. I made my way down to the orchard, where the girls lay in the grass. They seemed unaware of my approach, but I could hear their voices clearly.

I stopped and sat behind a tree when I heard Lily say, in a voice filled with anxiety, 'Uncle Eric told me that he had a surprise for me downstairs. He gave my brothers a game to play with and told them they mustn't disturb us. I ....'

'Shh. All is well child; I listen only to what you want to tell me. But it is good to talk. I tell the Witch my story and now I feel better.'

'He tied me up Nellie. He put a collar around my neck and he ... hurt me.'

'The Witch, she tell me what he did child. You have no need to speak of the horrors he did to you. These same things have been done to me.'

'I heard my Mummy yelling, 'He's killed her ... he's killed her.'

'Where was your Mummy and Daddy?'

'They went out to see somebody, I think. They weren't there.'

'Nellie a lady came. A shiny lady. She said I didn't have to stay, but then I heard Mummy yelling and the lady went ... and I got all confused, but I didn't want to stay Nellie ... so I left; but then I was here, and Sandy was picking me up.'

'You are safe child. No one will harm you here.'

They were silent for several moments. I made ready to leave when Lily spoke again.

'Why do you call Sandy a witch, Nellie? Can she do magic?'

'She has the magic of sight beyond the veil. Also, she can hear and speak to those of us this side of the veil. Most people would not be able to see us child. Not all of those who came before her could see as she does.'

'What is the veil?'

'It hides us when we can no longer dwell in our bodies. There are other veils beyond this one. I have seen them, but it is difficult to know what lies behind them.'

'But Nellie, I still have a body.'

'It is a memory only, little one. We cling to it because that is what we know.'

'Nellie does that mean ... am I dead?'

'Our bodies are dead Lily, our souls live on. There is another place we can go to if this is what we wish, but I have ... not gone. Fear keeps me here. You are innocent and have no need to fear what waits for you on the other side.'

'Do I have to go to the other side?'

'It is best. I think for some there is peace but not all.'

'Would there be peace for me?'

'Of this, I am sure.'

'Can't you come with me?'

'Some things we must do alone. You are brave, but I will stay with you for as long as I am able, have no fear.'

Amazed and reassured by Dardanelle's words, I gained my feet, left my hiding place behind the tree and made my way back to house. What I had to say could wait. There was no doubt in my mind now, that I had made the right decision to allow Dardanelle into the house.

I was sitting on the back steps, waiting for the girls, when I saw them make their way back to the house. The closeness between them was evident, and I wondered how Dardanelle would cope when it was time for Lily to leave.

Would she leave?

The thought triggered an alarm that began in the pit of my stomach and radiated throughout my body.

Surely Dardanelle's reluctance to leave, would not entice Lily to become one of the lost ones?

I pushed that worrying thought aside.

The girls stopped at the distance I had set for Dardanelle back when I had first seen her. Hands clasped together; they waited in silent expectation.

I sat in contemplation of them before speaking, 'Dardanelle, you must agree to two conditions first, before I allow you to stay in the house.'

'Her name is Nellie, now,' interposed Lily.

'Don't interrupt me, please.' I threw a censoring glance at Lily.

She compressed her lips into a thin line. Her eyes showed disapproval and defiance, which I may not have liked, but realised it was an improvement on fear and apathy.

I returned my attention to Dardanelle.

'Agree to stay in the second bedroom only. You do not have my permission to wander throughout the house, and especially not to come into my bedroom. Chance will tell me if you do.'

'I agree to whatever you say. I wish only to stay with the child.'

Lily's face had become radiant and hopeful, she bounced on her toes with anticipation.

'What is other condition?' Asked Dardanelle.

'That's it. Stay in the second bedroom and not wander. You can leave the house any time you wish.'

'I come now?'

I nodded.

The girls floated past me up the stairs. They were in the spare bedroom, before I stood to make my way up the steps to the verandah.

Spring came to an end, and the first days of summer arrived.

Dardanelle kept to her word. A peaceful energy surrounded the two girls. They spent less time playing and more time just being in each other's company, wandering the paddocks or laying in the grass, talking. They didn't include me in their conversations, I knew theirs was a connection that the living could have no part of.

Lily stopped eating and drinking, and I watched for signs of her impending departure.

If Dardanelle knew, she gave no indication. A seed of worry formed in the back of my mind. How was Dardanelle going to react when

Lily crossed? While I doubted she would go back to the angry young woman I had first encountered; I knew that Lily's transition would have a devastating effect on her.

CHAPTER THIRTY-ONE

Summer brought with it the memory of my arrival to the house. The year had gone fast. If someone had told me before I left home, that I would be harvesting potatoes from my own land, I would have told them they were dreaming.

Collecting vegetables, I had grown, seemed more unbelievable to me than living with ghosts. I had spent the last hour, digging up my vegetable plot with a garden fork and spade in order to unearth its bounty. Several dozen sweet potatoes lay waiting to be collected, washed, and stored. I had started on the white potato bed, when movement from Chance caught my attention, and I turned to see Rupert materialize beside me.

'You are needed. They are in the orchard,' he told me.

I'd removed my gloves, dusted soil from my clothes and was on my way even as he finished speaking. With swift strides and Chance loping gracefully beside me; I made my way to the orchard, and found the girls huddled against the log that I had sat on and ate oranges, the first day I arrived.

'Something is wrong, Nellie. I can feel it. You must tell Sandy,' I heard Lily whisper to Dardanelle.

'I'm here,' I said.

The girls scooted apart so that I could sit between them. I placed one arm around Lily. Chance settled on the log and snuggled into my back.

'Tell me what you feel,' I urged Lily.

'Someone is coming, and I feel ... I think it is time for me to leave,' she whispered. 'And I'm scared.'

She nestled closer to me. Her thumb moved to her lips, she mouthed at it anxiously before letting it fall, then scrambled onto my lap, burrowing into me. A deeper coldness touched my right side, as Dardanelle leaned against me for support.

I hugged Lily to me and whispered. 'A light will come soon but it won't harm you. It is your guide to the other side.'

'But I don't want to go. I want to stay with Nellie and you.'

'Nellie can go too, if she wants,' I told her.

I turned to Dardanelle who looked as if she was ready to flee.

'Don't leave. Please don't leave. They won't harm you, and Lily needs you,' I whispered softly to her.

Her lovely hazel eyes stared at me with such a blank expression, I knew it was taking every ounce of her courage not to disappear. She gave a slight nod of acknowledgement, and I breathed a little easier.

A band of silvery light shot with amethyst appeared and hovered in front of us.

I felt all of us startle backwards, the solid log and Chance at my back gave me a sense of support.

The streak of light gradually widened into an enormous ball of shimmering radiance; the globe separated into three distinct Beings. Each Being was three metres tall and pulsed with a vibrational energy that became so over-whelming my mouth fell open. Sudden tears leaked from my eyes and slid down my face.

Lily pressed herself so closely against my chest, it felt like she wanted to disappear inside me. On my other side, Dardanelle was making soft squeaking noises. While I felt nothing but love and peace emanating from the trio, my heart raced. By taking several deep breaths and letting them out slowly, I attempted to force myself to calmness, not only for my sake, but for the sake of the girls.

The Being standing before Dardanelle, opened her arms and spoke with a soft musical voice. I had visions of a tranquil breeze moving along the strings of a harp.

'Come home child, you have wandered long enough. Release your fear. Remorse has unchained you from the deeds of the past and we would welcome you home.'

I looked down at Dardanelle. She was staring at the Being with wide eyes and an entranced, but terrified expression on her face.

'Dardanelle? Did you hear what she, (*Was it a she?*) said?' I whispered.

While one part of my mind was functioning and coping with this unimaginable situation, another part was remembering Mum's words. '*I saw who and what came for them.*'

Is this what she saw as a child? No wonder she had been terrified.

Dardanelle turned her head slightly towards me, in an attempt it seemed, to keep one eye on me, and the other on the shimmering figures in front of us.

A slight nod told me she had heard, but how much she understood I wasn't sure.

'You will not be punished, Dardanelle. Go with them, you will be safe.'

'I will not ... burn in the fires of hell?' she whispered.

'On this side of the veil there is only love, but it is you who must decide. Come child, come home,' the Angel said spreading its arm wider in a welcoming gesture.

Dardanelle rose slowly to her feet and stood staring at the Spiritual Entity. She looked like she was ready for flight. I felt a moment of anxiety waiting for her to make her decision - towards or away from the light.

'Nellie? Don't leave me,' cried Lily in a trembling voice.

She twisted herself free from my arms to stand beside Dardanelle, then grasped her hand.

Dardanelle gasped, looking down at her hand, 'I can feel you.' She stared at Lily in wonderment'

'We can go together, Nellie,' Lily encouraged in a soft voice, pulling her towards the light.

Dardanelle allowed herself to be led and took a tentative step forward.

That small step symbolised an important decision, it drew them onwards and the two girls drifted inexorably towards the Angel standing in front of Dardanelle. As they moved forward, the light surrounding the Being expanded until it touched the girls.

Dardanelle and Lily vanished in a detonation of light.

CHAPTER THIRTY-TWO

Alone and sitting on the ground with the majestic Beings in front of me, I felt as insignificant as a grain of sand upon an enormous beach.

In a voice as equally musical as the first to speak, the middle Angel said, 'We thank you for your guardianship and offer you the blessing of Knowing.'

From her outstretched hand, a tiny ball of light floated towards me.

What!

I blinked and recoiled, feeling trapped now instead of supported by the hard wooden log at my back. Unable to move, I watched in fascinated alarm as the light came steadily on.

The Angel was speaking, but I was so fixated on the orb, I only heard every second word, '... need extra help, call ... who care for ... broken ... will come.'

The ball of light touched my solar plexus, and I felt a slow, sinuous warmth flowing through my body. It began as a tingle, then burst into a delightful euphoria, which ignited every cell of my being.

Time stood still.

When I opened my eyes, I was alone, laying on the ground under a darkening sky

How long have I been laying here?

Did I faint?

Chance was huddled against me, mewling like a kitten. Sitting up, I gathered him into my arms, and held his trembling body against mine. Strangely, I felt calm, though I wasn't sure I could stand, my legs didn't feel too steady.

Might be a better idea to just sit and wait.

I did sit and wait, until I felt Chance relax and my legs grow less wobbly.

Moving Chance from my lap to the ground, I used the fallen tree to haul myself backwards and up, until I was sitting on the log. After a few moments, I pushed myself upward to stand on trembling legs and assessed my ability to move.

Gradually, with Chance a black streak racing ahead of me, I made my way back to the garden. I'm not sure how long I stood staring without seeing the potatoes and the excavated earth.

Disparate images floated through my mind. The girls' laughter as they ran through the grass, chasing each other around the trees. Dardanelle, plucking at the grass, wanting so badly to feel again. The explosion of light taking them to the other side.

I need a drink.

The thought turned me towards the house. I came to awareness standing in the kitchen, holding the fridge door open. The fridge was empty and hot. There would be no electricity until the energy field surrounding the property changed.

I don't remember closing the door or moving out to the verandah and sitting at the table. Chance brought me back to the present by jumping on the table and rubbing himself against me. I rubbed along his back and massaged his ears. He purred with contentment.

'I need a hug too,' I told him, and thought of George, though I knew it would be unfair to go to him. He wanted so much more, and I didn't want to use him as a crutch. The time to tell George I was ready for a relationship would come but now was not the time - I had a lot to process.

I passed the next couple of days in a type of stupor, going about my days by rote. The potato crop needed harvesting but thoughts of Dardanelle's departure, and how miraculous it had been, started an avalanche of tears. The ground became littered with tissues as I worked slowly towards collecting the vegetables.

Having removed them from the earth, I set about washing the potatoes, and came to awareness standing still, staring at the blank wall of the laundry. Keeping my hands busy allowed my mind to wander unrestrained.

Imbedded into my psyche were the Beings of light.

Had I imagined them?

Of course not! Stop doubting yourself!

Recalling what Mum had told me, '*I saw who and what came for them,*' triggered an onslaught of grief and sobbing so overwhelmingly strong, it left me exhausted.

At other times, I would be in the middle of some mundane chore, like washing the dishes, to find my nose dripping snot, with tears flowing down my face.

Ultimately, I decided I was having a stress reaction and needed to give myself time to accept all that had happened.

The death of my parents, and the move to Violet's Place, had sparked a significant transformation in the way I saw myself. I had gone from being what I thought of as a normal everyday kind of person, to one who was able to witness the transition of life from form to energy. My understanding of life had evolved in ways I could never have imagined.

Eventually, I understood that the body was a gift; without it we would not have the capacity to experience love, hunger, pain, pleasure or the many other myriad emotions that humans are capable of.

Instead of trying to keep busy to distract myself, I walked in nature, absorbing its calmness and strength until the last vestige of turmoil and pain within me subsided.

Rupert didn't come as I'd hoped he would, there was much I wanted to talk over with him.

A week went by, the electricity came back on. I refilled the fridge and stopped myself thinking about George by keeping busy.

A few good night's sleep recovered my equilibrium. Chance and I continued taking long walks in the bush, which enabled me to maintain the sense of calmness at the centre of my being.

Another week disappeared into the ether; I allowed thoughts of George to enter my mind. It was time to go to him and tell him that I loved him.

CHAPTER THIRTY-THREE

I emerged from my bedroom early the next morning, to see George entering the kitchen from the back door. Dressed in jeans, T-shirt, and thongs, he was cleaner than I had ever seen him. Obviously, he hadn't come from working in the paddocks. My heart raced at the sight of him, suddenly I was nervous and full of doubts.

It's been so long!

Will I know what to do?

What if he thinks I'm a terrible lover?

Does my breath smell of coffee?

Our eyes met and locked; his dark eyes, full of love and desire forced all my fears into the background of my mind. Several heartbeats later, I kicked my shoes under the nearest chair.

Moving to George, I held his face between my palms, 'I love you and I'm sorry it's taken me so long to say it.'

Standing on tiptoes, I kissed him softly on the lips. He drew back, his searching gaze held mine for several seconds before he gathered me into his arms. Our lips joined, and we shared a deeper more passionate kiss.

George broke our contact. 'This is real. You're sure?'

'I'm sure. We need to talk about so many things, but right now talking is not what I want to do.'

Stepping back, I slowly undid the buttons on my blouse; removing the shirt, I dropped it in the direction of the chair. I didn't check to see if my aim was sure. My hands moved to the zip of my jeans. George's eyes followed my every movement; he stayed still as if frozen to the spot.

'How much do I need to take off, George?'

My question seemed to wake him from his inertia, he scooped me up in his arms and carried me back to my bedroom.

Over his shoulder, I saw Chance heading for the verandah.

George and I spent the remainder of summer getting to know each other better. He held me close when I cried and told him of Dardanelle and Lily. With the telling, the last of the pain and tension I held was released.

George spoke of his plans for the farm, and his wish for a family. I knew the moment had come, when I had to tell him what had been troubling me subconsciously, about entering into a relationship.

'I will continue on with my work ...,' I paused.

I hadn't considered it my work or my vocation - or destiny, call it what you will, until that moment; but I knew with certainty, that I would continue providing a place for souls to transition.

George studied me for a prolonged thought-filled moment. 'I have, very carefully, considered the possibilities of how we would negotiate your relationship with the dead. After my many talks with Vivienne, I know how much she regretted giving up the love that produced your mother. I decided not long after we met that if by some dumb luck, I would ever entice you not only into my bed but into my life, I would never ask you to choose.'

Tears of gratitude stung my eyes as I leant across and gently skimmed George's mouth with a kiss.

He grabbed me. Our bodies connected, and the gentle kiss transformed into passionate lovemaking.

Christmas came, Chance and I arrived at the farm to be greeted by Jack and Sally. The dogs knew immediately that Chance was in charge, and a wary but tolerant relationship developed between the three.

George and I spent the day relaxing on the banks of, or swimming in the river flowing through his land. Afterwards, we shared a picnic lunch under a thick canopy of river gums and paperbark trees.

The new year began a change in routine for us both. George and the dogs joined Chance and I at Violet's Place. Every morning before returning to his farm to work, George would make me breakfast. In the evenings, I ran his bath and cooked dinner for us both.

Our bubble lasted until the end of summer.

Sitting on the back verandah, with breakfast finished, we were discussing our plans for the day when Rupert appeared beside us.

'Bloody hell, Rupert! You could have given us some warning!' I gasped, putting my coffee cup down on the table with a thud.

He lifted an eyebrow, shrugged his shoulders, and removed his pipe from his shirt pocket. The pipe was lit, and I wondered how it didn't burn a hole in his shirt, until I remembered he was a ghost. He put the pipe in his mouth, and gave a few satisfying puffs, before removing it and pointing it at George and me.

'This has never happened before,' he informed us. 'If you intend to remain as the guardian,'- he pointed his pipe at me then at George - 'you will not be able to live here permanently.'

George and I glanced at each other; while we had not discussed details, we both knew we wanted our relationship to work more than anything.

'Rupert, we'll work it out,' I told him. 'And I do intend to remain as guardian.'

How is it going to work?' George didn't say it aloud, but I heard the words in my mind with the widening of his eyes and the questioning look on his face.

'We'll work it out,' I told him softly. Then to Rupert in a stronger voice, 'We *will* work it out Rupert.'

'Then you must know that George cannot stay here when the visitors come,' cautioned Rupert. 'Neither can the child that is coming, except of course the guardian-heir.'

Guardian-heir! Interesting way of putting it.

'That's not going to be anytime soon. So, stop worrying,' I told him firmly.

'I'm not worrying,' replied Rupert. 'I'm delivering a message.'

'A message? From ...? Why would ....?' I was flabbergasted and couldn't seem to finish any of my sentences.

Why would they be interested?

At least my thoughts were coherent.

'Consider the message delivered, and you don't have as much time as you think,' said Rupert mysteriously before putting the pipe back in his mouth. He puffed on his pipe contentedly, while giving us a knowing look with a definite twinkle in his eye.

What had we missed?

'Out with-it Rupert,' George said in a firm voice, he obviously had had the same thought. 'What are you not telling us. You look like the cat who's got all the cream.'

Chance chose that moment to jump on the table. He sat and groomed his paws while staring at Rupert; it seemed like he wanted to hear too.

'Hang on a minute,' said George. 'You said the child that *is* coming. Do you mean *now?*'

I didn't think Rupert's grin could get any wider or more annoying, but it did before he abruptly disappeared.

Speechless, George and I sat staring at each other across the table.

'That, changes things,' said George.

I shook my head, 'No, it doesn't. What does it change?'

'You can't stay here, pregnant and alone.'

'George! Vivienne and all my ancestors stayed here, pregnant and alone.'

'Yes ... but ...' he spluttered.

As if sensing the growing friction, Chance leapt from the table, gracefully moving down the stairs and out into the yard where Jack and Sally greeted him affectionately.

I touched my abdomen in awe, I had often dreamed what it would be like to carry a baby, but the truth was, I didn't feel any different.

What had Rupert said?

Was this child the guardian-heir? No something in the way he phrased it - what had he said?

And what did he mean that this had never happened before?

'Bloody hell!' said George. 'What are we going to do? I don't want you ...,' the look I gave him stopped him mid speech.

I kept my voice calm, even though I could feel the tension building. 'You said you were ready for this, George.'

'Yes, I know. You're right. I did. I guess it was just something I dreamed about, never thinking it might come true. It's too soon.' Shock and disbelief was clear in his voice.

George looked around wildly, ran his fingers through his hair. 'A *baby!* Crikey, I'm going to be a father. I know what I said. I meant it too, I don't ... didn't want you to make a choice, but the reality of it is different.'

'George, stop!' I told him firmly. I realise you are worried, but Lily and Dardanelle have convinced me that the dead need me, or someone like me, and there doesn't seem to be anyone else. I ...,' I stopped.

George was looking at me as if I had two heads. His face had turned red and started to swell. I thought he was going to explode.

'You think the *dead* need you? Forget about the bloody dead. I need you! Our child needs you!'

Where had the man, who only a few weeks ago, told me he wouldn't expect me to make a choice, gone?

If steam could have come out of my ears, it would have. And his too by the look on his face.

'Why does it have to be one or the other? Why can't it be both?' I said, in what I'm sure was a reasonable tone, though I wondered if he could hear my teeth grinding together with the effort it took.

'You want a foot in both worlds?' George stood and glared at me. 'Our child will need a full-time mother, and I want a wife, not a ... a ... part-time one who also wants to be an intermediary for the dead. NO! NO! I WON'T HAVE IT!'

Struggling to contain the hurt I felt, I said in the coldest voice, I could manage, 'Well you didn't think about this enough. Did you? Just what did you imagine was going to happen?'

George gulped. 'I didn't think it would happen so soon, the baby I mean. I thought we would have time. I thought you ….'

'You thought I would give it up? Were you lying when you told me ….'

George interrupted me mid-sentence, 'Well, it seems to frighten and upset you ….'

'It did, it does.' I interjected, neither of us were able to finish our sentences without the other interrupting. 'That's what I was trying to explain to you about Dardanelle and Lily. They made me change my mind. I don't want to stop. Not yet anyway. Maybe there will come a day when I do, but that isn't now.'

How could I stop? This isn't something you just walk away from.

'If not now, then when?' said George through gritted teeth. His intense stare reminded me of a lion stalking its prey. 'What about the baby?'

As if I could forget about the baby! I took a deep breath, losing my resolve not to yell.

'YOU'RE its father. YOU can take care of it when I can't.'

'So, it's an *it* now, is it?'

I raised one eyebrow at him. He was being ridiculous.

'Okay. Okay.' He held up his hands as if in surrender.

'You do know one of our children will be the next guardian? Do you want her to walk into this as unprepared as I was?'

A lightbulb switched on inside my head.

'That's what Rupert meant!' I exclaimed. '*This* child is not the next guardian! That's what has never happened before. One pregnancy … one guardian.'

A shocked look spread across George's face. 'Oh! I didn't ... of course ... my child the next guardian. How can we possibly prepare her?' His voice was almost a whisper.

I relaxed and stopped myself from grinning when I heard the plural 'we'. I waited and watched George's mind process the idea, that his daughter would be the next guardian. But this one wasn't, had he understood that yet?

He grabbed the chair as if for support then slumped back into it. He stared with eyes so glazed they appeared not to be able to see anything. Not uttering a word, his fingers drummed the table. Abruptly, he slammed his palm downwards and glowered at me.

'You're right. Of course, you're bloody right, but that doesn't mean I have to like it.'

A sudden coolness filled the air around me. George seemed unaware, but I knew what it meant. The timing couldn't have been worse. I studied George, wondering how he was going to react.

'I'm going to get another visitor soon George. It's best you don't come back tonight.'

'*Now*? Someone is coming *NOW*? This is what it's going to be like isn't it? We're going to be in the middle of something important and you ... you're going to leave me to it. Just like that!' He snapped his fingers and glared at me. 'Or are you using it as an excuse? No. I course you're not .... Sorry.' He looked ashamed of his ungracious thought.

He stood then, drew me to my feet and held me firmly in his arms.

'Sorry, love, sorry,' he whispered into my hair. I had a different vision in my mind on what my future family life would look like. It's hard to let go of an old dream.'

'You'll have to create a new one,' I mumbled into his chest, wrapping my arms tightly around him.

His grip relaxed. He held me gently before slowly letting me go. His gaze roamed my face as if trying to imprint it on his mind.

'I can't believe I'm going to be a father. It's like a dream and a night-mare all wrapped into one.'

'We'll work it out George.' I held him with a firm gaze until he slowly nodded.

CHAPTER THIRTY-FOUR

It was nearing midday before my new visitor arrived, with a thud, on the front verandah. She lay in the same spot as John and Lily, which I finally figured out must be the entry point, even though Jann and Fred were in the back yard when I first saw them.

Short and stout with curly grey hair and a round motherly face, she appeared to be in her seventies. Pale and looking very dazed, she lay unmoving. I sat beside her and waited until the groggy look in her eyes cleared, and movement returned to her limbs. Unsteadily, the woman raised herself to a sitting position.

'Who are you?' The voice was harsh, and not at all in keeping with the maternal image her appearance portrayed.

There was an underlying viciousness to her tone, that had me retreating behind formality. 'My name is Sandrine. And yours is?'

She turned her head slightly to gaze sideways at me. 'Jean,' was the rather abrupt reply.

'Would you like help to stand, Jean?' I asked.

'Of course! I can hardly stand by myself,' she sniffed.

I cupped one hand under her elbow.

Oh! God! She's ... ugh!

Nausea twisted my stomach in knots, and it took an enormous effort not to recoil from touching her. Jean's energy was repulsive. Fighting confusion and my own instincts, I helped her to her feet and guided her to one of the chairs on the back verandah.

She slid into the chair and sat resting her head in her hands for several minutes, before looking at me and asking, 'Where am I? How did I get here?'

'Would you like a cup of tea or water?' I asked.

She studied me with eyes that sent a shiver down my spine. Green marbles would look softer.

'Tea,' and after a pause long enough to be considered rude, she added, 'please.' Then, in the same unpleasant manner, repeated her earlier questions, 'Where am I and what am I doing here?'

'Have you had an accident?'

'An accident? I suppose I did, if you could call being pushed off a bloody ladder an accident.'

'Who pushed you?'

'What business is it of yours, girl, and how many times do I have to ask, what am I doing here?'

She was rude, repellent and perplexing. I decided the only way I could get this woman's attention, was to hit her (figurately speaking) between the eyes.

'You're dead, otherwise you wouldn't be here. This is where souls, who have died suddenly, come before they pass on.'

The look Jean gave me was pure scepticism. There was no doubt in her mind, I was lying. She started laughing and laughed so hard I thought she was going to fall off the chair. Laughing turned to hiccoughs, then to anger.

'Don't yank my chain girl, or I'll give you what for. How can I be bloody dead if I'm sitting here talking to you. Are you dead?'

I clamped my jaw clamped shut, and managed, with a great deal of difficulty, to maintain a calm exterior. The woman's energy was off. I didn't like her, and she was obviously trouble. Not sure what to say or what my next move was going to be, I sat and contemplated her.

What in heavens am I going to do with you? I'm not even sure I want to ....

The thought was interrupted by Rupert suddenly appearing beside me, and a flash of hissing, spitting, growling black fur. In one fluid movement, Chance had leapt onto the table and launched himself at our new visitor. His attack on Jean was so sudden and ferocious, she was knocked backwards off her seat and regained her feet only sufficiently enough to scramble away on all fours.

Chance's impetus was not slowed by Jean's fall; he leapt onto her back, claws unsheathed, and by the screams coming from her, digging in deeply.

Sparing Rupert a quick surprised glance, I leapt to my feet, yelling, 'Chance! Stop!'

As only a cat can do, he jumped straight up in the air and backwards all at the same time, and landed at my feet, facing Jean. Fur and tail erect, the growl in his chest deepened. While I was dillydallying over what I was going to do, he had made up his mind what to do with Jean - and that helped me make up my mind too.

On unsteady legs, Jean pulled herself to her feet. Clutching the verandah railing for support, she made her way over to the corner before turning and facing us.

With eyes blazing hatred at me, she said, 'You and that blasted cat just made a very big mistake.'

Moving her glaring gaze to Rupert, she demanded, 'Where the hell did you come from? It looked like you just appeared out of nowhere. And who the hell *are* you?'

Rupert's demeanour of silent watchfulness appeared to make her uneasy, she turned her attention back to me.

Quietly, I said, 'You can't stay here. I am going to call someone to come and get you.'

I wasn't sure why I told her that. An inner knowing perhaps, and the comfort of having Rupert beside me, but I was sure of what I was doing.

Jean's laugh had no humour in it, and she looked at me with contempt.

'You've both picked the wrong woman to mess with.'

'Come and get her, or I will banish her. She cannot stay here.' I said in a firm voice that fell just below a yell.

'Who are you talking to?' Jean looked around, then back at me.

Suspiciousness filled her eyes. 'You don't look like you're a six-pack short of a carton, but I suppose you never can tell,' she sneered.

Turning her vile attention to Rupert; her voice coloured by scorn, she said, 'What do you think you're going to do, you skinny, pathetic, old codger. You look like a strong wind would blow you over. I could take you with one hand tied behind my back.'

Her viperous attack was interrupted by the arrival of an Entity, who wasn't anything like the three who came for Dardanelle and Lily. His energy was definitely male, whereas I was still undecided about the others. Neither was he accompanied by a beaming white light. The light that surrounded him, was dark blue laced with strands of red and yellow. He gave the impression of coiled power waiting to pounce.

Shock replaced the sneering look in Jean's eyes. A heartbeat later, fear replaced surprise. She stepped back and held on tighter to the railing.

Levelling a laser gaze at Jean, in a deep voice filled with authority, the Entity commanded, 'Come.'

Uncertainty filled Jean's face, she glanced at me, then back to the Spiritual Being. Gone was her hate filled attitude.

In that moment, I realised Jean responded positively to someone she considered more powerful than herself. The look she gave me was filled with dawning respect. The unwavering glare I returned, should have told her I didn't need or want her respect.

Jean took a deep breath, licked her lips, and smoothed her dress with hands that shook. Her attempts to soothe herself appeared to work, she squared her shoulders and straightened her spine. All in an effort it seemed, to stand tall and convey a confidence I was sure she no longer possessed.

With infinitesimal steps, Jean walked towards the Angel. Before she reached him, a door abruptly opened in front of her, and her next step took her through a portal. As the door closed behind her, I heard a soft gasp, followed by a quickly suppressed scream.

'You have no need of me now,' said Rupert, waking me up from the entrancement of watching the terrifying new Entity order Jean to step through a portal to heavens knew where.

'What! Don't leave m ...,' He was gone before I could finish the sentence.

Bloody man!

I was left alone with the Emissary. His cool, silent, observation told me I was being weighed and measured. Forcing myself to stillness, I suddenly understood Jean's need to soothe herself.

His voice, powerful and authoritarian when speaking to Jean, became soft and musical. I thought I heard chimes. 'You are as powerful as they say. I am pleased to be of service,' he said, dipping his head to me.

I had no time to respond, ask questions or even thank him. He disappeared as silently and as swiftly as he came.

CHAPTER THIRTY-FIVE

Like Jean, I moved on shaky legs to the railings and clutched them for support. Chance came and offered his support by twining himself through my legs.

'Good job, Chance.' I told him.

Radiating self-satisfaction, he sat and licked his paws, before washing his face. Chance stayed with me until I thought my knees would function properly again, then he found a spot on the verandah to sunbathe.

I lowered myself to a seat, with scattered thoughts flooding my mind.

Bloody Angels! Was he an Angel?

Bloody ghosts! Why did Rupert leave?

There's nothing powerful about me.

What did he mean by that?

Why was he different to the others?

Whatever he was he was certainly scary. More importantly, how did I know to call him?

I needed answers and yelled, 'Come back here Rupert! I want to talk to you!'

When he appeared, I told him, 'It's about bloody time you came when I called, and why did you *leave* me?'

I was surprised he came. He didn't usually.

'There was no reason for me to stay,' he told me calmly. 'Why do you need an explanation when you already know the answers? Your instincts are, it seems to me, perfectly intact. I am somewhat mystified by your need to apply logic *and* have someone else to tell you that you are right.'

My mouth fell open at his calm reasoning, I closed it with a snap. His insight was annoyingly correct. I did feel the need for someone else (namely him) to explain the inexplicable, and to tell me I was right.

'Okay. Okay! You're right. What can you tell me about that … Being?' I was still unsure what I should call them.

Rupert shrugged, 'Never have I seen one like him before. But then souls like that woman, don't usually come here, so that's new. Must have something to do with your strength.'

'My *strength*?'

What was he talking about? Or was that another thing I would have to discover for myself. Since I'd nothing to compare my strength to, it was going to be extremely difficult.

'What was your father like?' Rupert's voice interrupted my musings.

'Cold. Distant. Unreachable.'

'Yes. Well, since all those words mean basically the same thing, all it really tells me is that you and he didn't have a very good relationship.'

I rolled my eyes. 'That's putting it mildly,' I told Rupert, dryly. 'I have no idea what Mum saw in him. The way she talked about how he was when they first met, it seems like he was a totally different person to the one I knew.'

'People change, and sometimes they change back to who they really were in the first place.' Rupert said enigmatically.

He took his pipe from his pocket and sucked briefly on the empty bowl. Removing it from between his teeth, he waved it around and remarked, 'You need to learn that, for a lot of this, there is no explanation. Or at least not one we are privy to.'

'And *you*,' an extra thrust of the pipe at me, 'must accept what is, and trust that you *know*. You heard what those three who came for Dardanelle and Lily said?'

'You weren't there.'

'Of course I was,' he told me scornfully.

Maybe he was, I was too overawed to know if someone else was present or not. I decided to indulge him.

'They said they gave me the gift of knowing, but I didn't understand the rest, I was too overwhelmed, my hearing didn't seem to work.'

He nodded, 'I thought so. They gave you the gift of Knowing and told you that you could call for help for difficult souls. And you did, without any prompting from me. So, a part of you did understand.'

Another point of the pipe. 'It's in you girl.'

'Humph,' was all I could think to say, and changed the subject. 'I assume she went to some place other than where everyone else I've encountered has gone.'

'Yes, she needs extra help. It also means she will return to this realm sooner; she has a lot to learn.'

'Oh? I thought you didn't know much.' I couldn't resist.

'What I know, and what I'm prepared to, or need to tell you, are two different things.'

His attention then went to filling his pipe, tamping the tobacco down and lighting it before taking several satisfying puffs. For a ghost he appeared incredibly solid.

'How did you come to be a part of this, Rupert?'

He eyed me, over the top of his pipe bowl, with raised brows.

'I wondered when you would get around to asking that question.'

I waited in silence. He puffed on his pipe. There was no doubt in my mind, he was trying to figure out exactly what and how much he was going to tell me, if anything at all.

In a voice filled with wistfulness, Rupert gave me a glimpse into his past. 'I was like Dardanelle once, a lost one. Angry with the world as I understood it. With myself, and most of all with the woman I loved and a boyhood friend, who betrayed me. I refused to cross until I met Violet. Like you, she was powerful and also like you, she had an infinite amount of patience and love. When I finally did cross over, I asked to return as a caretaker to the guardians.'

He shrugged, puffed on his pipe, then added, 'Of course, in the beginning it was simply to be near Violet. I have been here ever since. Like you, I have found my path.'

There was a world of pain and love in his story, so I simply said, 'Thank you Rupert for sharing that with me.'

He nodded and said, 'Time for me to go.'

Kind of him to declare it, he usually just vanished.

For several minutes, I sat on the verandah, staring into space, so much had happened it was hard to process. To channel my thoughts in another direction, and to give my subconscious mind time to deal with the events of the day, I made my way to the kitchen. With a fresh cup of coffee beside me, I picked up the book I was in the middle of reading and allowed it to take me to someone else's reality.

CHAPTER THIRTY-SIX

When I wasn't pondering my astonishment at being pregnant, loving George, Rupert's story, Jean's vileness and the Angel who came for her, I spent the next two days waiting for George to return. He would know the property wasn't shielded. Why hadn't he come?

Expectation became concern and morphed into anger, until I was stomping around the place, muttering 'Bloody George!' at random intervals and watching vainly for his arrival. If I happened to pass Chance while stomping and muttering, I received a swipe from an unsheathed set of claws that seemed to be telling me to relax. The wounds weren't deep but tiny spots of blood dotted my ankles. I became very adept at spotting him in time and manoeuvring myself out of his way.

On the third day, realising I needed a different perspective, I headed into Balford.

The footpaths were crowded. People with busy lives, forgetting to take a moment and simply breathe, forgetting (or not wanting to believe) that death dogged their every footstep.

The noise of many engines and their overpowering, nose contorting, scent of petrol fumes assailed my senses. I stood in the middle of life and realised that this was what I had forgotten. A connection to life and the lives of the people around me. In a moment of clarity, I knew I needed to balance the isolation of shepherding the dead, with immersing myself into the flow of life, and all its complexities.

But what did that balance entail?

A life with George's as a farmer's wife, with its many and no doubt conflicting demands. As well as raise a family with its own array of varying and complex difficulties.

Where did that leave guiding the dead?

If the child I was carrying was not the guardian-heir, who would look after her in my absence? George couldn't, not full time.

Recognising that I stood at a crossroads, and one that I had blundered into due to a lack of mindfulness, was overwhelming. I wandered the streets without purpose, wanting desperately for a resolution to float to the surface of my mind.

Instead, my thoughts harped: *George is right, you're going to be in the middle of something important, and the dead are going to call you away.*

You can't have it all, said that annoying voice that sometimes popped, unbidden, into the mind.

Of course I can, I just have to work out how. I reassured it and ignored the fact that I was once again arguing with myself.

Outside a hair salon, remembering days long gone of regular visits to the hairdresser, I resisted the temptation to make an appointment I was unlikely to keep. Reluctantly I moved on. My hair had grown in the past year, and I wore it now, more often than not, in a ponytail; occasionally trimming the ends with a pair of kitchen scissors.

A sense of loss flowed through me and came to rest in my centre. Allowing it to settle and recognising it as one of many losses, I walked the streets until I found a bookshop and spent a pleasant half hour choosing several books to add to my small library. George also liked to read. Books were one of the many things that connected us; we had spent countless evenings together, reading in harmonious silence.

Even as I wandered, my mind nagged: *You can't be sure you would be able to keep a hair appointment, how are you going to manage a family, and take care of the dead?*

This is what Vivienne had faced, and she walked away from the one she loved.

Should I walk away?

But this child is not my replacement, she cannot live at Violet's Place.

Either I had to leave the care of the child almost totally to George or leave the dead to find their own way.

So what? Dad lived in the same house as Mum and I, but he might as well as lived somewhere else for all the involvement he had in our lives.

On and on my mind babbled, I walked the streets trying without much success to shut it down.

In a dress shop changing room, the green silk dress I had chosen slid smoothly over my head and shoulders, caught at my hips and drifted slowly downwards to rest just beyond my knees. Sensual pleasure flooded my body, my skin tingled with excitement. Immediately, I thought of George and my heart raced, small pants of desire escaped my lips.

Stop! I shook my head to clear it, my breathing slowed, returning to normal.

I gulped and caressed the soft material where it nipped at my waist and examined my reflection in the mirror. Very soon my waistline would disappear, and I would have no need for a dress like this.

Discarding that insight as a future worry, I bought the dress and left the store thinking I would wear it for George's next visit. It's time he saw me in something else other than jeans and shirts that were showing their age.

What was I thinking! Looking sexy for George, that's what got me into this mess.

Why had I assumed that just because Robert and I couldn't have a baby, then George and I wouldn't be able to too. Ridiculous thinking!

Or maybe it was hope that lived inside of me. The hope that George and I, against all the odds, could make our relationship work.

My mind had started its harping again.

'Sandrine!' A voice called.

I turned to find Harriet behind me. 'Are you coming to see me?' She asked.

'Oh! Harriet! I wasn't, but of course I must. So much has happened, I had forgotten all that I had asked you to do. I'm so sorry.'

Her gaze roved over me for an instant. 'Well, I must say you are looking wonderful. So much better than when I last saw you. So, whatever you are doing, keep doing it. What are you doing now?'

'Well, I was going to find somewhere to have lunch.' I told her.

She glanced at her watch, 'Come to my rooms in, say half an hour. I'll organise some lunch for us to be brought there, and I can get you up to date with all you want or need to know. How will that be?'

'That will be fine, Harriet. I will see you there,' I told her trying not to grin.

It had sounded more like an order than an invitation. She hadn't changed, so I must have, because once I would have been annoyed by her imperious attitude.

'Very good,' she said, moving past me and continuing on her way.

Dutifully, I arrived at Harriet's office at the appointed time, to find not only Harriet but Beatrice Milledge, Jill, John's mother and two strangers.

'We will get down to business eventually,' Harriet greeted me in her usual no-nonsense way. 'But first, I want to introduce you to your support team. And before you say anything, let me tell you, you do need one. Out there on that isolated property with only the dead for company, I've decided that you need to be reminded of life.'

'Uh,' was all I could manage. Life! Babies and relationships. Dealing with the dead was easier.

'This is Carol, Jill's daughter.' Harriet introduced a young woman close to John's age. Though she looked very much like her mother, her demeanour was cheerful and outgoing. Jill's reserved air of sadness lingered in her expression and manner.

I nodded to Carol who bounced over and engulfed me in a welcoming hug.

'Did you really see John?' Her voice was loud in my ear.

'Ah. Yes. I did.'

'That's enough, Carol. Let the poor girl breathe, there will be enough time later for your questions,' interrupted Harriet before turning me to the other young woman. 'And this is Hilary, Beatrice's granddaughter.'

Hilary was the antithesis of Beatrice's staid, no-nonsense attitude. The youngest member of the group was long, lean, tattooed, and had rings attached to her nose, belly button and ears but none on her hands. She eyed me with cool scepticism conflicting with avid interest.

'I'm pleased to meet you both,' I said automatically, receiving reassuring nods from the older women.

'Right, now that the introductions are over, let's eat.' Harriet gestured towards a table, where a variety of dishes and refreshments were laid out.

I had no sooner filled my mouth with food, when Carol bombarded me with questions, 'Tell me about John. Did you see him pass? Who came for him? Was he sad? What did he tell you? What did you say to him?'

Answering all their questions as best I could, I drove home two hours later, in a mood that bounced between being happy and being conflicted. Happy with meeting new friends, and overwhelmed with gratitude for their support, and the knowledge that there were people in my life I could call on in times of need. Potential babysitters too, should I require them. Conflicted, because now it seemed I had to choose between having a family and shepherding the dead.

I wanted both.

CHAPTER THIRTY-SEVEN

The following morning, I stood in front of the mirror examining my reflection. The silk dress I'd purchased was beautiful. I felt feminine and sexy; it was both my armour and my ammunition.

Today, I was going to visit George and attempt to determine if he and I would merge our lives together or go our separate ways. Either way, we had the difficult task of co-parenting a child.

The sound of a large vehicle making its way up the driveway and stopping near the house, interrupted the study of my reflection and my thoughts. From the back door, I watched George exit his truck and make his way to where I stood.

Suddenly nervous, I attempted a welcoming smile and said softly, 'Hello, George.'

Desire filled his eyes. 'Crikey! You don't make it easy for a man,' exclaimed George.

Inwardly my smile widened. As being sensible was the order of the day, I prevented the smile from showing on my face, and asked, 'Why have you brought the truck? You don't usually.'

'I've come to get Lavender; she needs to go to the bull. You'll need milk next year. I figure when her calf gets old enough, we'll rotate them so that they each calve every second or third year. I'll bring them both back when she's in calf.'

My inward smile died; my heart raced. Had I already lost him.?

'You ... you're bringing them back? What ...?'

'You're staying here, aren't you?' He interrupted. Desire was still in his eyes, but it was at war with an emotion I didn't recognise.

'Yes, I am.' I told him. 'But ....'

'That's what I figured. That's why I haven't come to see you. I needed to work things out in my own head. I had to figure out what I needed, what you needed, and how we can make things work. Or even if we could make it work.'

'I want to make it work, George.' The words rushed out of me.

So much for seduction. I was starting to feel a little desperate, and very close to crying. 'I need to stay here. I can't leave. I....'

'I know that.' He interrupted me again. 'That's one thing I was pretty sure of. You wouldn't be able to leave. I've decided to get a cottage built on the property, and we'll employ a farm hand and his wife. An older couple who've had their family, and who will be happy to fill the gap when we're not available.'

'Oh! George ... George,' I whispered, tears of gratitude and love flooded my eyes.

'I've forgotten what I'd rehearsed,' he gulped. 'Seeing you in that bloody dress has chased it out of my mind.'

Music to my ears. This time my smile was evident and very wide. Happiness flooded my being.

'It basically boils down to this. We *will* work this out,' George was adamant. 'Whatever comes, we will handle it together. We'll re-write the whole bloody book on relationships if we have to. All that matters, is that I love you, and I want you and the baby in my life.'

'Oh! George,' I laughed. 'Only you could be so practical and so romantic at the same time. Of course, we'll work it out. I love you so much.'

'Right. Now that that's over, let's get this bloody dress off you. Thank you for wearing it, but all it does is make me want to get you out of it and into bed. I've waited long enough,' he growled softly, striding towards me.

Such a long wait, all of fifteen minutes.

CHAPTER THIRTY-EIGHT

On autopilot, my feet carried me across country, as the crow flies, towards the farm and my family. I'd eschewed the five-minute drive, in favour of a six-kilometre walk in order to release pent-up tension and clear my head.

Chance knew where we were going and ran on ahead. Excitement had obviously got the better of him. Occasionally, he stopped and looked back, or waited until he saw me, then off he would run again.

My visitor had gone, and I needed the respite of the farm and the company of my family more than ever. Flora Hutchinson's stay had been a nightmare, and my mind replayed, over and over, our last encounter.

Sitting on the verandah with the remnants of breakfast on the table before us, I told her of the difficult decision I'd made during the night.

'If you don't leave, I'll have to banish you.' I told her.

'You can't banish me,' she scoffed.

'She can.' Rupert told her. He'd arrived early, settled into the comfortable chair I had purchased for him and puffed contentedly on his pipe. His support encouraged me to do what I must.

Flora sniffed, scepticism showing clearly in her eyes and face. 'Look at me. I'm ninety-eight years old and frail. Where am I going to go?'

'The body you once resided in was ninety-eight years old. Your spirit is free and as you well know; you may transition at any time. So, stop pretending to be something you are not.' My tone was harsh, but I no longer cared.

On numerous occasions, over the past month I explained to her that as she no longer needed me, her presence kept me at the house and divided me from my family. All of which she'd ignored, disparaged, or played the victim card, making this confrontation, long overdue.

As usual my, no longer welcome, visitor thought she knew of another way to change my mind.

'My grandmother told me she knew that someone had stayed with one of the Legg women for many years. I don't see why I can't do the same thing.

Mum's decision to flee, and leave me without the knowledge of previous generations, often came back to haunt me. In the beginning I'd felt sympathy for her but oftentimes now, it was difficult to shake the resentment that flared within me, especially since we had both lived a miserable life with Dad.

While I couldn't refute this manipulative old woman's claim, I certainly wasn't going to allow that to be the reason for her to stay.

'Be that as it may, you are not staying here any longer. Call them or I *will* banish you.'

'I'm not going anywhere. I have company. I'm well looked after. I have more now than I've had for a very long time.'

That was because you drove everyone away with your demanding neediness.

The thought rested in mind, unexpressed. I studied the woman in silence. Despite being ninety-eight years old, Flora had the emotional maturity of a teenager. She'd backed me into a corner and now I had to say words I thought I would never say, and that once said, would hurt my heart.

'Flora Hutchinson, you are banished from this house, this property and my proximity. I banish you, Flora. Go, and return only when you are prepared to cross the veil.'

Astonishment resided briefly on her face before she faded and was gone.

Rupert stood, surveyed me with eyes full of sympathy and pride before he too disappeared.

I was left alone with the enormity of my decision weighing heavily on my mind. Needing a hug, I headed for the home of George's arms.

The walk helped to clear my mind of guilt and doubt, and I opened the door to the farmhouse keen to embrace my husband and daughter.

'Mummy! Mum ... my!' Three-year-old Elodie hurtled toward me. I scooped her up into my arms and twirled her around.

Her little arms clung to my neck and George embraced us both.

I was home.

'Tough one, huh? You look terrible.' He whispered in my ear.

I nodded and lifted my face in search of a kiss. George willingly complied with a kiss that held a promise of waiting passion. I sighed and he grinned.

Elodie squirmed and I put her down. She grabbed my hand.

'June has babies, Mummy. Come see.'

Before I left a month ago, June, a hen belonging to George's flock, had been flying over the coop to freedom. We suspected she had been hiding her eggs, and it seemed we were right.

'Are you alright?' George asked, sotto voice.

'It was Flora Hutchinson.' I told him. Naming an elderly woman well known in the Balford community.

'Bloody hell! Tough one.'

I nodded to let him know I'd heard. Elodie tugged at my hand, urging me to follow. 'Come, Mummy.' She led me out to the yard.

Chance already had the chickens in his sight and was stalking them.

'Leave them, Chance.' I told him. He gave me a side eyed glance and sat to give his paws an unnecessary inspection.

Elodie let go of my hand and toddled over to the hen and her eight chickens.

George gathered me into his arms, and I clung to him, glad to be back home.

'You feel so good.' He whispered.

'You feel even better. She was horrible. I had to banish her.'

If George was surprised, he gave no indication. He never judged or commented on the decisions I made regarding the visitors.

'Where is Grandpa Wupert?' Elodie had lost interest in the hen and her chickens.

'He'll come in a couple of days, honey. Mummy needs a rest.' George lifted her into his arms. She stretched towards me, and he transferred her to my arms.

George's assessment was correct. While Rupert loved being part of a family and was a frequent visitor to both homes; he would be giving me space to recover from my decision to forbid Flora to stay at Violet's Place.

'I'll have to visit Flora's family and pay my respects.' I told George.

'Plenty of time for that. She's been gone a month, and she wasn't mourned.'

George was right. Violet's Place required a thorough cleansing. I needed a rest and to reconnect with my family. Everything else could wait.

Elodie struggled from my grasp and was off. Born at the farm three years ago on a cool night, late in winter, she had begun exploring, the moment walking became more than teeter tottering about on chubby legs.

After her birth, the three of us shared seven glorious months together on George's farm, until the day came when I sensed Violet's Place pulling me back. Tearfully, George and I said our goodbyes, knowing that the idyll was over, and the hard work of the decision we had made, was beginning.

Elodie was nine months old when I saw her again. George and I cried and hugged each other close. The two months since we had seen each other and seemed like an eternity.

'Her hair has changed colour.' I remarked.

Elodie's baby blonde hair had darkened to the colour of George's hair.

George nodded, 'She has your eyes, but that's about all.'

I grinned at the pride in his voice. George looked sheepish and shrugged.

Crawling over to the kitchen table, Elodie grabbed hold of its leg and pulled herself upright. With the aid of the furniture, she explored the room.

I gasped, 'She's walking!'

During my absence, Elodie had taken her first step. So much to miss out on. My heart still aches when I think of all that I missed.

A few weeks after I'd banished Flora, well rested and at peace now with the decision I had made, it was time to pay a visit to her family.

The journey into Balford wasn't without misgivings. I'd delayed my visit to Flora's children as long as I could.

'They have to be able to express how they really feel.' I told George when he offered his support. 'They won't if you come with me, they'll see you as my protector, even if they don't consciously realise it.'

'I *am* your protector.' He growled.

I kissed him and said, 'This is something I must do alone.'

Only one of Flora's four children wanted news of their mother. Felicity Jones eyed me from the other side of her kitchen table. Well-groomed with her white hair in a neat bob, she was not her mother's daughter. In response to life's tests, Flora had chosen immaturity and expected others to take care of her. Felicity had faced her trials head on and grown into a woman comfortable in her own skin.

'Would you like another cup of tea?' Had been her only response to the story I felt compelled to tell her.

I shook my head, and we sat in silence for several moments before Felicity spoke again.

'What you have told me, doesn't surprise me. Thank you for coming. You didn't have to. You are very brave.'

There was an air of indefinable sadness about the woman. I gained a vague sense of how difficult it must have been, being the daughter of someone who was incapable of mothering.

'Can I help you in any way?' I asked

'How does your husband cope with the work that you do?'

It was an abrupt change of subject and startled me for a moment. Nobody had asked me that question before and I took a moment to answer her. 'George thinks the visitors are a nuisance and an interruption to our lives. He is right, but I see them as part as life itself.'

Felicity nodded, whether in agreement or acknowledgement, I couldn't tell but it encouraged me to continue.

'I see life and death as two sides of the same coin. I believe they are intertwined and inseparable, and a reminder that life must be cherished.' I paused, not sure how she would react, then threw caution to the wind. 'I mean, how else can we, as beings of energy experience life, but through a body?'

Her eyebrows lifted in surprise. 'That's how you see us. 'Beings of energy?"

'Are we not?'

Her silence indicated she was turning the idea over in her mind. Eventually she said, 'No. I would argue that most people would see themselves as a body that may or may not have a soul.'

Not having a reply, I asked, 'May I have another cup of tea?'

Felicity obviously needed to talk.

She refreshed my teacup, and said, 'What about your family, dear. You've just told me my mother stayed with you for a month and would've stayed longer if you hadn't had the courage to send her on her way. That was a month you didn't spend with your family.'

She was very perceptive. I took a deep breath, sipped my tea and considered my answer carefully. 'Yes, it can be very hard. It's hard to tell how Elodie feels, she's always happy to see me and has all the resilience and adaptability of a child. George is wonderful, he never says a cross word and always welcomes home.

'Then you are lucky. Now, my dear. Go back to your family, they have more need of you than I do. And forget about my mother. No-one could help her, because she was never prepared to help herself. Whatever you do - don't feel guilty.'

CHAPTER THIRTY-NINE

I'm having twin boys, George,' I told him one morning over breakfast, during one of his and Elodie's visits with me.

He spluttered, the mouthful of tea he had just taken, all over the table, some landing on my plate. Serves me right for not having better timing.

'Right. Well, don't think you're not having antenatal care this time around. I'm making an appointment as soon as they're open.'

When pregnant with Elodie, George wanted me to deliver in a hospital. Much to his chagrin I refused. 'There's no need for hospitals, or health care with this baby, George. She is going to be fine. And so am I.'

My reassurances counted for nothing, he grumbled all the way through the pregnancy, right up to the moment he held her in his arms and welcomed her into the world.

'It's a bit early,' I told him. 'They won't do a scan yet nor will they believe me when I tell them I'm having twins.'

'Too bloody bad. You're going in.'

George bundled Elodie and me into the car and drove to the doctor's office that day. Since I already knew the boys would be born early, and have breathing problems, I allowed him to have his way, and to think he was in charge.

A month after their birth, when we finally got them home, in stark contrast to Elodie, the boys carried within them an ocean of calm. With dark hair and eyes, Daniel and James were the image of George.

'I can't believe they're already sleeping through the night,' observed George three weeks after we got them home.

'I know, they are so much more laid-back than Elodie.' I agreed.

'When can I play with them, Mummy?'

'Soon, love. When they are bigger. They're too small yet.'

Without Elodie's energetic restlessness, from the beginning, they were more relaxed, gentle and placid, and would spend their days observing the world around them.

'It's been blissful without visitors,' remarked George one evening after we had lived together for a year as a family at Violet's Place.

I sighed, 'It's been wonderful. I've been lucky enough to watch the boys take their first steps. They love stories and books and most of all they love their big sister. I hope this will last a while longer.'

It was not to be, a few days later reality intervened. With a heavy heart, I waved goodbye to my family; they returned to the farm, and I was left alone with the dead. As privileged as I am to watch some souls depart, I am mindful of the need to value the ones who have been placed into my care. At times, I am filled with pain, when I think of the days lost with my family, and the milestones I have not celebrated with them.

'WHY DON'T YOU HAVE a T.V. Mummy?' complained four-year-old James on one of their visits.

'Yeah. We want to watch Dr. Who,' agreed Daniel.

'The electricity is unreliable here. It doesn't always work. Not only that, I also don't want a T.V.' I told them.

They threw me an identical grumpy look and wandered outside. While their first love was all things science fiction, it wasn't long before they were engrossed in their second love of climbing trees. Another love was following Elodie. Her restless roaming over the five hundred acres of George's farm would often include two boys, two dogs and sometimes a cat, as she set off on her explorations of the countryside.

The twins were five years old when I became pregnant for the third time.

'I'm pregnant George. Our lucky last and the guardian.' I told him one morning as we lay in bed at Violet's Place, listening to our children play, not so quietly, in the second bedroom.

'Shh. Mum and Dad are asleep.' Elodie told the boys in a not so soft voice.

George turned on his side to face me. With eyes full of love, he smoothed the hair off my face and looped it around my ear.

'Do you need to see a doctor?'

I supressed a grin and placed a soft kiss on his nose. *He is learning.*

'No. We are going to be just fine.'

George didn't see the ghosts of guardians past who surrounded us six months later, as the baby slipped from between my thighs. All his focus was on cutting the cord and welcoming his new daughter in the world.

'Hello, Victoria,' he whispered, as he swaddled her and held her close.

Victoria's dark hair and green eyes were her only resemblance to Elodie. Quieter, self-contained and observant, her first word, not surprisingly was, 'Wupert'. He and the children shared a special bond, and it was obvious he loved being part of our family.

One day, after preventing her desperate attempts to follow Elodie and the boys on one of their excursions into the bush, we were comforting her and drying her tears when George asked, 'When can Vicky take over do you think?'

'George, she is three years old,' I laughed. 'It'll be at least another twenty years, if not more.

Grey streaks had been added to hair and beard. He had retained his catlike walk, though his figure was no longer as lithe as it once was. If it were possible, I loved him more now than I had when I first fell in love with him.

'Do you ever regret ...,' I couldn't finish the sentence

'What?' He asked softly, then in sudden understanding, chuckled.

'Do I regret all this magnificent chaos?'

I nodded mutely.

'Never. Sandrine, when I chose you, when I chose us ... I chose love, and I can never regret that,' said my wonderful man.

THE END

ACKNOWLEDGEMENTS:

To my friend, Joy Rains for being my first reader, your comments helped to develop the very rough copy of 'Violet's Place' into a more rounded story.

To my daughter, Jenny, co-editor, and excellent proofreader, for your attention to detail, and for being part of the story's development. And, as always for your continued support and belief in my creative abilities.

To my daughter Cathy, book cover concept extraordinaire, formatting aide and all-round supporter.

To Sarah Lewin a fellow author, for your superb editing, your encouraging comments and support, and for writing the back blurb for me, a task I always find difficult.

To Elizabeth Rimmington, also a fellow author for your encouragement, advise and frustration at my overuse of ellipses. You'll be happy to know that I took care of most of them.

To Sophie and my fellow writers at the Writers Group I attend for the insightful comments which helped to develop some of my sentences.

www.ingramcontent.com/pod-product-compliance
Lightning Source LLC
Chambersburg PA
CBHW020520120726
47904CB00003B/910